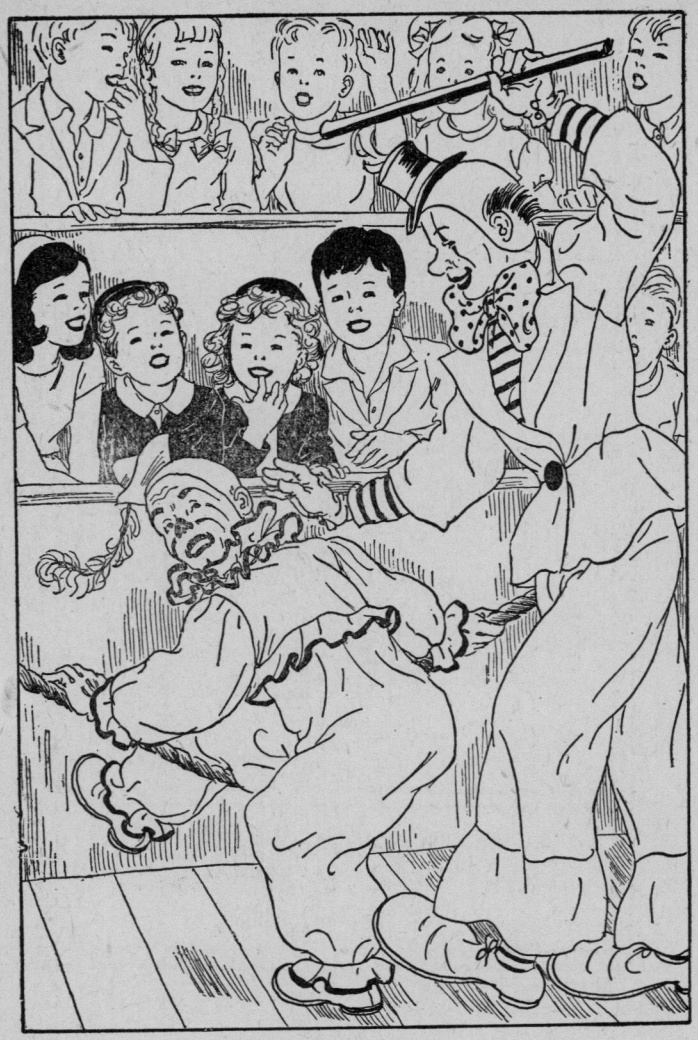

"I've got you now!" cried the tall clown.

The Bobbsey Twins at the Circus

The Bobbsey Twins at the Circus

BY

LAURA LEE HOPE

AUTHOR OF "THE BOBBSEY TWINS SERIES,"

NEW YORK
GROSSET & DUNLAP
PUBLISHERS

CONTENTS

THE BOBBSEY TWINS AT THE CIRCUS

CHAPTER I

DOG TRICKS

"COME here, Bert!" called Nan Bobbsey to her twin brother. "See what Flossie and Freddie are doing."

"Oh," answered Bert from the side porch, "I guess they're doing what they're always doing, playing some game. Anyhow, I can't come just now, Nan."

"Why not?"

"I'm fixing my fish-pole. John Marsh and I are going to try to catch a few. I'm busy!"

"Oh, please come here!" begged Nan, and her voice sounded so eager and excited that Bert paused in his work of oiling the reel on his fish-pole and asked in a loud voice:

"Can't you tell me what they are doing instead of having me jump up and go there to see? Can't you tell me?"

"I'd rather have you come here and look," Nan answered. There was laughter in her voice, but this was not unusual when she spoke of Flossie and Freddie, the smaller Bobbsey twins. Flossie and Freddie often did things to make Bert and Nan laugh. "Come, Bert, do, please!" his sister begged. "Oh, it's too funny for anything."

"All right, I'll come!" Bert said with something like a sigh of resignation, the kind brothers often give when they agree to do what their sisters have coaxed them to do. "Only if it isn't funny you don't catch me again. I must hurry to get this pole fixed. I told John I'd meet him at 9 o'clock and it's almost that now."

"This won't take you a minute," went on Nan. "Do hurry before they stop it!"

"Well, what are they doing?" asked Bert as he laid aside his fishing tackle and started around the corner of the house. "Can't you tell a fellow?"

"Well, I'll tell you, since you're coming

now," Nan answered. "But I want you to see it. Flossie and Freddie are making that new dog—the one which came here the other day —they're making him stand on his head."

"No!" cried Bert, scarcely believing what his sister said. "No!"

"Yes they are, truly!" murmured Nan, her voice still eager.

"A dog can't stand on his head, that is, not exactly on his *head*," Bert objected. "Maybe he can stand on his front paws and——"

"Well, that's just the same as standing on his head, or almost," Nan said. "Anyhow, that's what Flossie and Freddie are doing— making that new dog do tricks."

"That's funny," went on Bert as he joined his sister at the back of the house. "I thought that new dog was only a mongrel. I didn't think it could do tricks."

"I didn't, either," agreed Nan. "But it seems he can."

"Flossie and Freddie must have been teaching him," declared Bert. "Those twins are smarter than I thought they were to show a stray dog a trick, like standing on his front paws, in a few days."

"Maybe," remarked Nan, "the dog knew this trick all the while, and Flossie and Freddie just found it out."

"Maybe," assented Bert. "But it's funny if a trick dog should stray away from where he belongs and come to us."

"Well, this dog seemed to be a stray," said Nan. "Anyhow, he came here the other day, when you were visiting over at Charlie Mason's—the time you went on the hike—and Flossie and Freddie got some scraps from Dinah and fed him. Then they teased Mother to let them keep him."

"It's queer if Mother let them keep a dog," murmured Bert. "She said, after Snap went away the last time, and didn't come back, that we never could have another dog."

"I know she said that," murmured Nan, "but Flossie and Freddie teased so hard to keep this dog that Mother let them. And maybe Snap will come back again. You know he often goes away and stays maybe a week or two, and then he comes back. So does Snoop, our dear old cat."

"Yes, I know," said Bert. "What's his name?"

"Oh, I don't believe he has any name yet, unless Flossie and Freddie have given him one," answered Nan.

"Well, where is he?" asked Bert. "I don't see any stray dog nor the twins, either."

"They're right behind that bush," explained his sister in a low voice. "You can't see them from here. I noticed them when I was coming back from the store, but I kept quiet so I could tell you. Come on, walk down this path and you can see them."

Taking hold of Bert's hand to guide him, and putting her finger over her lips as a signal for silence, Nan led her brother down toward the end of the garden back of the Bobbsey house. As Bert neared the place he could hear the voices of his brother and his other sister. He could also hear the barking of a dog.

"There they are!" whispered Nan. "See them?"

"Sure!" murmured Bert.

He and Nan now had a good view, through a screen of bushes, of Flossie and Freddie. The small twins were kneeling on the grass and between them was a small dog, of the fox-terrier kind, and black and white in color.

"He's a lot cleaner than when he first came here," went on Nan. "I guess they washed him."

"Who?" asked Bert.

"Flossie and Freddie," explained Nan. "I saw them out in the garage one day with a pail and a lot of soap and water. They probably washed the dog."

"They're clever," admitted Bert, "but I don't see them making this dog stand on his head," he went on. "He's just sitting on his tail. That's no trick. I knew there was a catch in this somewhere. I'm going back and fix my reel."

"No! Please don't!" begged Nan. "I want you to see this. Truly, when I called to you the dog was actually walking around on his front legs. Standing on his head, I call it. But you were so long coming that maybe—"

"Hush! Wait a minute!" interrupted Bert.

As he spoke, he and Nan saw Freddie take hold of the stray dog's hind legs and gently lift them up in the air. At the same time Flossie called:

"Come on, now, be a circus dog!"

As if waiting for this signal the dog suddenly gave a little jump, raised his hind legs higher, and in a moment was doing the trick of standing on his head, or, as Bert said more correctly, on his front paws.

"See!" exclaimed Nan. "What did I tell you?"

"Say, he *is* doing it!" agreed Bert, smiling. "I didn't believe it at first but I do now. I wonder if he can do any other tricks?"

He started toward the little twins and their new pet, but Nan caught him by the arm and whispered:

"Wait a minute! Don't spoil it by going there now. Let's wait and see what else they do."

"All right," Bert agreed.

Hiding back of the screen of bushes he and Nan watched. Flossie and Freddie were giggling happily as their dog walked around the grass in a circle, his hind legs held well up in the air.

"Isn't he cute!" murmured Flossie.

"He's more than cute!" Freddie said. "He's a smart dog. And he's mine!"

"Oh, you said I could have half of him,"

objected Flossie. "I helped you wash him and I got some scraps from Dinah for him. Can't I have half?"

"Well, which half do you want?" asked Freddie.

"The half nearest me," Flossie answered, and she drew a line with her finger down the middle of the dog's back, the long way. The dog was now standing on all four legs, having done his trick enough—at least he probably thought so.

"You can't divide a dog in half that way!" objected Freddie.

"Why not?" asked Flossie.

" 'Cause," her brother replied, "you got to divide him this way," and he drew a line across the dog's back, midway between the head and tail. "Always you make halves of a dog that way," said Freddie. "And whoever takes the head half has to feed him."

"Then I'll take the tail half," decided Flossie, for she remembered that when she had to feed old Snap, she often had to give up part of her play hour to do it.

"All right," agreed Freddie. "Then if you have the tail half, you'll have to wash the dog. All right, I'll feed him and you can wash him."

Flossie was not quite sure that she had made such a good bargain after all, and there was such a funny look on her face that Bert and Nan could not help laughing in their hiding-place back of the bushes.

"Who's there?" called Freddie quickly.

"I know, it's Nan and Bert," said Flossie.

"Oh, come and see our trick dog!" invited Freddie. "He's real smart—better than Snap. Come and see him do tricks!"

Thus discovered, Bert and his sister walked toward the smaller twins, the new dog wagging his long tail in a friendly way as he saw the older children. So far Bert had not paid much attention to the newcomer. Now he patted its head and stroked the smooth, clean back as Flossie remarked:

"He's half mine and half Freddie's. I own the tail half and I'm going to wash him when he gets dirty."

"Where'd this dog come from, anyhow?" asked Bert, noticing that the terrier was really a nice animal.

"He just came," Freddie answered. "First

we didn't know he was a trick dog, but he is."

"How'd you find it out?" asked Bert.

"Why," explained his small brother, "I just sort of took hold of his hind legs a little while ago and lifted them off the ground. Then all of a sudden Waggo gave a jump and started to walk around on his front legs. It's a good trick, isn't it?"

"Fine!" Bert agreed. "Is that his name— Waggo?"

"Yes," stated Flossie. "I named him that on account of the way he wags his tail."

"All dogs wag their tails," Bert said, looking more carefully at the small twins' pet.

"But not the way Waggo wags his," Freddie said. "Go on, Waggo, wiggle your tail!" he ordered, and as if waiting for this command the new pet wagged his tail not only from side to side, but up and down and around in a circle.

"Just like an egg-beater!" chuckled Flossie.

"What a funny thing to say!" murmured Nan.

"Well, an egg-beater goes around," declared Flossie. "Anyhow, he's a good trick dog and the tail half is mine."

"This surely is queer," observed Bert, still patting the dog. "I wonder if he will do the trick for me?"

"He will if you tell him to be a circus dog," said Freddie.

"All right," spoke Bert. Then to the dog he called, "Be a circus dog!"

At once the animal began to walk on his front legs.

"Isn't he cute!" murmured Nan.

"I just love him!" said Flossie.

"If we had Snap now," said Bert, "maybe he would learn to do tricks when he saw this dog. I wonder where Snap is? Has either of you seen him this last week or two?" he asked the small twins.

"No, he hasn't come back since the last time he ran away," said Freddie.

"And Snoop, our nice old cat hasn't come back, either," went on Flossie. "He went away about the same time Snap did. Maybe they're both dead," she added sadly.

"Nonsense!" exclaimed Nan. "Lots of times, after Snap and Snoop have run away, we've thought they might be dead. But they always came to life again."

"I wish they'd come to life now, and then we'd have two dogs," said Freddie.

"And if Snoop would come back we'd have two cats," went on his twin sister.

"Oh yes, the Christmas cat that had kittens in our cellar," agreed Freddie. "Well, we have her yet, but her kittens are all gone. If Snap comes back, and Snoop comes back, we'll have a lot of animals. But we're not going to keep this dog," he went on, pointing to the new animal.

"No, we aren't going to keep Waggo," agreed Flossie.

"What are you going to do with him?" Bert wanted to know. "Take him back where he belongs?"

"We don't know where he belongs," Freddie stated. "We're going to teach him a few more tricks, and then we're going to sell him to the circus."

"What circus?" asked Nan.

"There isn't going to be any circus here!" said Bert.

"Yes there is, too!" cried Flossie. "Tell him

what we saw, Freddie. We know about the circus and you don't," she went on, laughing and shaking a finger at Nan and Bert. "We were going to keep it for a secret but we'll tell you. The circus is coming here and we're going to sell our trick dog to it and make a lot of money, aren't we, Freddie?"

"Sure we are!" was the answer, and Bert and Nan wondered what was coming next.

CHAPTER II

THE DISHPAN DRUM

BERT BOBBSEY looked at his sister Nan and Nan Bobbsey looked at her brother Bert. Both the older Bobbsey twins were much surprised, not only at seeing Flossie and Freddie making the strange dog do the trick, but also at hearing what the smaller twins had said.

"What's all this about a circus?" asked Bert.

"I believe they're just pretending," remarked Nan. This was not surprising, as Flossie and Freddie often played at this game.

"Oh, we aren't pretending at all!" exclaimed Flossie. "Are we, Freddie?"

"Not a bit!" and he shook his head hard. "Here, give us a paw!" he ordered the dog who was now sitting on his tail, as you might say.

At once Waggo held out a paw which Freddie grasped.

"Oh, that's another trick!" cried Nan. "Isn't he clever!"

"I guess he knows a lot more tricks," Flossie said.

"Sure he does!" agreed Freddie. "We'll get a lot of money for him from the circus!"

"Stop fooling and tell us about the circus!" suggested Bert. "I don't really believe one is coming," he added in a whisper to Nan.

"Yes there is!" cried Flossie, who overheard this. "Tell him, Freddie."

"Well," began the small Bobbsey boy, "when Flossie and I were coming back from downtown a little while ago, we took the short cut across the lots."

"And we saw 'em putting up the tents!" cried Flossie, unable to keep quiet any longer, though it was not very long since she had spoken.

"What tents?" Nan asked.

"Circus tents!" cried the small twins together. Then Freddie went on:

"We saw the men putting up posters and we saw 'em bring up a lot of horses and some wagons, but we didn't see any animals."

"Nor any elephants," added Flossie.

"Then it can't be a circus," Bert decided. "It may be some sort of a traveling show but it isn't a circus or else there'd be elephants. There's something wrong."

"There must be," agreed Nan. "Anyhow, if there was going to be a circus there'd be a lot of posters up all over town, pictures of elephants and other animals and performers on the trapeze and things like that. We haven't seen a single poster."

"That's right," murmured Bert, and then he held out his hand and Waggo shook paws with the older Bobbsey boy, much to his delight.

"They started to put the posters up when Flossie and I were coming back from downtown," declared Freddie.

"What were you two doing downtown?"

"We went to buy a collar for Waggo," admitted Flossie, "but they cost too much so we didn't buy any."

"I'll make him one out of an old strap," said Freddie.

"What about this circus?" persisted Bert. "It's funny if one has come to town without posters being put up ahead of time."

"I don't see how it could happen," Nan remarked.

"There was an accident," Freddie explained. "Flossie and I heard some of the circus men talking about it. They weren't coming here to Lakeport until later, but they had a break-down or something, so they had to come here, sort of surprised like, I guess, and that's why they're just putting the posters up now. They're going to stay here two or three days."

"Oh, well, if they had an accident and came here ahead of time," said Bert, "I guess it's all right about the posters not being up until now. But this is going to be great! A circus! I'm going!"

"So am I!" cried Nan.

"We are, too," announced Freddie, speaking for himself and Flossie. "We're going to sell our trick dog there!"

"I guess none of the fellows know about this circus yet!" went on Bert. "I'm going to tell 'em. We'll have a lot of fun and maybe we can carry water for the elephants and get free tickets. Wow! This is dandy!"

The thoughts of the coming circus took the

twins' attention from the trick dog for a moment. Then Nan said:

"Let's go into the house and ask Mother if we may go to the circus!"

"Come on!" cried Flossie.

She and her twin brother, as well as Bert and Nan, started for the back door, which was the nearest one. Waggo seemed to know where the children were going and bounded off ahead of them.

The trick dog reached the kitchen first, leaping up the back steps. The screen door was closed but not hooked and, as the children watched, Waggo thrust one paw in through a small crack and pulled the door open for himself.

"Say, there's another trick!" cried Bert. "This dog is clever! I'm going to teach him more tricks!"

"He's our dog!" Flossie insisted, "and I own half of him."

"I own the other half!" declared Freddie, "and we're going to sell him to the circus and get a lot of money."

"We'll see about that," murmured Bert. "Maybe it will be better to keep him and teach him more tricks and get up a circus of our own."

"That would be wonderful!" murmured Nan. "If our old dog Snap would come back, and Snoop, our cat, and if we keep the cellar cat that had Christmas kittens, we'd have a lot of animals."

"Sure!" said Bert.

By this time Waggo had made his way into the kitchen. The four Bobbsey children were climbing up the steps to follow, when all of a sudden there was a loud cry. It was the voice of Dinah, the fat, jolly, Negro cook. Dinah was crying in alarm:

"Stop it! Quit! Git outen mah kitchen. Leave mah dishpan alone! Oh! Oh! Oh, look at him!"

"What's that?" cried Nan, startled.

"It must be some new trick Waggo is doing!" exclaimed Bert. "Come on!"

While the children are rushing into the kitchen where Dinah is uttering her warning cries, I will take just a few moments to tell my new readers a little about these jolly children.

There have been a number of books printed

telling about Bert, Nan, Flossie and Freddie. The first volume is named "The Bobbsey Twins," and tells of the good times the four children had at home with Snoop, Snap and many girl and boy friends.

As you have guessed, there were two sets of Bobbsey twins. Bert and Nan, the older, had brown hair and brown eyes. Flossie and Freddie had light hair and blue eyes. All four twins were lively, full of fun and liked to play and have adventures.

They lived with their father and mother in the eastern city of Lakeport, on Lake Metoka. where Mr. Bobbsey owned a lumberyard. Dinah, the Negro cook, and Sam Johnson, her husband, who cut the grass, washed the automobile and did work about the house, were almost as much members of the Bobbsey family as were the twins. When Flossie was smaller her father often called her his "little fat fairy," and in the same way he called Freddie his "little fireman," because the small boy was so fond of watching the engines rumble down the street.

The Bobbsey twins had many adventures by themselves or with their playmates in the country, at the seashore, in and out of school, at Meadow Brook, on Blueberry Island, at Cherry Corners and Spruce Lake, and you will find books telling about these happenings.

The story just before the one you are now reading is called "The Bobbsey Twins' Wonderful Secret," and has to do with a dear old cat who brought her kittens into the Bobbsey cellar at Christmas time. There was also another part of the secret that I am not allowed to tell you just yet.

Christmas had come and gone, and it was now Spring and the Bobbsey twins were ready for more good times. Then, most unexpectedly, the stray dog had come to the house and had been claimed by Flossie and Freddie.

Now this same dog Waggo was doing something in Dinah's kitchen which caused that jolly, fat cook to utter strange cries.

"What's he doing?" exclaimed Bert as he rushed up the steps ahead of his brother and sisters. "What's Waggo doing?"

"Jes' yo' come heah an' see, Honey Lamb!" called Dinah. "I nevah see sich a dog in all mah born days! Nevah! Stop it! Stop it, I say! Oh, yo' rascal!" she shouted, and then she laughed so the Bobbsey twins knew it could not be very serious.

They heard Waggo barking! Then they heard a strange, thumping sound, a rub-a-dub-dub sound. Dinah called again:

"Get away from mah dishpan!"

"What's he doing to the dishpan?" asked Freddie, for he was behind Bert and could not see. "What's Waggo doing?"

"He's done made a drum of mah dishpan, that's what he's gone an' done!" chuckled Dinah. "I nevah see sich a dog in all mah born days! Nevah!"

By this time Bert was inside the kitchen and he had a view of what was going on. It was surely a strange sight and Bert could not help laughing with Dinah. The other Bobbsey twins also laughed when they tumbled into the room and saw what was happening.

In the middle of the floor was Dinah's large, tin dishpan. The pan was standing on edge, tilted against the stove where Dinah had set it after washing and polishing it. She had left it there to dry while she did some other work. Waggo had rushed into the kitchen and there he stood, thumping his tail against the tin bottom and making a drum of it.

Dub! Dub! Rub-a-dub-dub! Waggo's tail was not cut short, as are those of many such dogs, so it was long enough to wag and strike the dishpan drum.

"Look at him! Look at him!" cried Dinah, laughing so hard that her fat body shook, as Nan said later, "like a cup of custard when you jiggle it."

Rub-a-dub-dub! Waggo drummed on the tin dishpan.

"This is a regular circus trick!" cried Bert. "I guess this dog knows a lot more stunts than we thought. He's valuable. We can get a lot of money for him!"

"We'll sell him to the circus!" cried Freddie.

"Oh, no! Let's keep him!" suggested Nan.

"We'll have our own circus!" suggested Flossie. "I'm not going to sell my half of Waggo! Never!"

"Now yo' let mah dishpan alone!" cried Dinah, still laughing. "I've got t' wash it all over, now yo' been thumpin' it! Git away, dog!"

She reached down to pick up the pan, and as she did so Waggo made a jump at her.

"Look out! He may bite you!" cried Nan.

CHAPTER III

THE CIRCUS GROUNDS

WAGGO was not the kind of a dog that bites. He was very gentle. But he surely looked as if he might bite as he leaped up at Dinah, who was bending down to pick up her dishpan. Though Nan had cried out in alarm there was really no danger.

"Stop it! Stop, I done tole you!" cried Dinah. "Let me alone! Git away!"

"What's he doing to Dinah?" asked Flossie, who could not see as Freddie had moved in front of her. "What's Waggo doing?"

"He's kissing Dinah!" Freddie answered.

"I hope he won't bite her," murmured Nan.

"No. He's only licking her face with his tongue," explained Bert. "I guess he's hungry."

"He needn't think he's goin' t' eat me!" declared Dinah, as she picked up her pan and hurried across the room. "I likes dogs an' cats an' sich, but I don't like 'em t' kiss me!"

"Well, he was kissing you all right!" chuckled Freddie.

"Oh, I wish I'd seen it!" said Flossie in disappointed tones. "You got right in my way, Freddie Bobbsey, and I couldn't see it at all. Go on, Dinah, please stoop down again so Waggo can kiss you some more and I can see it!"

"No indeed, Honey Lamb!" said Dinah, using one of the pet names she had given the twins. "I done had 'nuff kisses from a dog! Git away from me!" she ordered, as Waggo seemed ready to follow her around the kitchen. "Git away!"

"Sit up, Waggo!" commanded Freddie.

The animal obeyed at once, sitting up on his hind legs with his front paws drooped in front of him.

"Why, that's another trick!" exclaimed Flossie.

"It surely is!" agreed Bert. "This is a smart dog!"

"That isn't much of a trick," Freddie said. as if he knew all about dogs and their ways. "Lots of dogs," he went on, "can sit up like that and beg. But not many dogs can stand on their heads or drum on a tin dishpan."

"You're right," Bert said. "This must be a valuable dog and whoever lost him will give a lot of money to get him back. We'll advertise in the paper and get the reward."

"No!" said Freddie determinedly. "This is my dog and I'm going to sell him to the circus."

"He's half mine," Flossie objected. "We found him together and you said I could have half of him, Freddie."

"Yes, he's half yours," her small brother agreed. "But you said we'd sell him to the circus."

"Yes, I said it," assented Flossie. "And we will."

"No!" exclaimed Bert. "This is too valuable a dog to sell to a small circus. We'll advertise him and get the reward."

"No!" cried Freddie.

"Yes!" insisted Bert.

The Bobbsey boys were having a dispute and their voices were loud. Waggo dropped to all four paws and stood looking at the boys, his head cocked on one side.

"What's this? What's this?" asked Mrs.

Bobbsey, suddenly opening the door from the butler's pantry. "What's this loud talk about?"

"It's about Waggo," Nan explained.

"I'm going to sell him to the circus," Freddie explained, "and Flossie and I will divide the money. He's our dog!"

"Mother," exclaimed Bert, "this is a valuable trick dog. We've just found out he can do lots of tricks."

"He drummed on Dinah's dishpan," Nan said.

"And he tried to kiss her but I didn't see it 'cause Freddie was in the way," broke in Flossie. "Dinah won't let him do it again so I could see but I wish she would!"

"My! My! Such a lot of talk!" exclaimed Mrs. Bobbsey, laughing. "And such a dispute! I don't like that."

"Well," went on Bert, "I don't believe Freddie should sell this valuable trick dog to a circus. It ought to go back to the owner and maybe we'll get a reward."

"If it's such a valuable dog, certainly the owner ought to have him back, reward or not," Mrs. Bobbsey said. "But what's this about a circus? I did not know one was coming to Lakeport."

"We didn't either, until just now," Bert said. "Flossie and Freddie say they saw the men putting up the tents. We were coming in to ask if we might go when we heard Waggo drumming on Dinah's dishpan."

"Can the dog really do that?"

"Sure!" said Freddie. "Here! I'll show you!"

He went to get the pan, but Dinah said:

"No, yo' can't hab dat! Heah, take dis ole pan, it's jist as good fo' a drum!"

She let Freddie take another tin pan and when it was set on the floor, Waggo, without being told, trotted over to it and began to thump the bottom with his tail.

Rub-a-dub-dub! The Bobbsey Twins looked on in wondering admiration.

"He is like a circus dog," Mrs. Bobbsey said. "I think you had better let your father decide what is best to do with him. Do you know who owns him?"

None of the twins did, and Flossie and Freddie explained how one day, about a week before, the dog had trotted into the yard where they were playing and had made friends with them at once. Since then he had seemed to consider the Bobbsey house his home. The small twins had fed their new pet with scraps Dinah had given them.

"I didn't pay much attention to him until today," Bert said, "or I'd have seen what a valuable dog he is. But it wouldn't be right to sell him to this circus that's coming, would it, Mother?"

"I hardly think so," Mrs. Bobbsey answered.

"But he's our dog, Flossie's and mine," insisted Freddie, "and we want the money."

"If nobody claims this dog after we advertise him," said Bert, "we may keep him. Then we can make a lot more money, maybe, by getting up a circus of our own than we can by selling Waggo to this traveling show that's coming."

"You can't make a circus with just one dog," objected Freddie.

"We have the Christmas cat," Flossie reminded him.

"That won't be enough, either."

"No, it won't," Bert agreed. "But if we

could find Snoop and Snap we could train them, maybe, and I could do some tricks, and Flossie and Freddie can sing, and Nan, you can jump rope—Oh, we could get up a good circus."

"But we haven't Snap and Snoop," Freddie said. He did not want to give up the idea of selling Waggo and getting money quickly.

"Snap and Snoop can't be far away," Bert declared. "They're always wandering off and staying away for a week at a time. But they often come back and the next time they come we'll keep 'em shut up until we can train 'em for our circus."

"Well, all right," Freddie agreed, though not very willingly. "But Waggo is half mine and half Flossie's."

"Let it go that way," Bert said with a laugh. "Anyhow, you surely have a valuable trick dog. I wonder what other tricks he can do?"

"Don't try him in Dinah's kitchen," suggested Mrs. Bobbsey. "She has her work to do. Take Waggo outside and when your father comes home from the office we'll talk to him about what is best to do."

"May we go to the circus, Mother?" asked Bert.

"I'll see," was all Mrs. Bobbsey replied.

"Come on!" cried Bert to his brother and sisters. "Let's go out and look for Snap and Snoop! I'll ask the fellows if any of them have seen our old dog and cat."

"And we'll see what new tricks Waggo can do," added Freddie.

"Maybe I ought to wash him," Flossie suggested.

"No," decided Freddie, "not now. A wet dog can't do tricks as well as a dry one. But I can feed him!" he exclaimed as an afterthought. "Have you any scraps, Dinah?"

"Heah, take 'em an' please git out ob mah kitchen!" begged the fat cook.

The Bobbsey twins, accompanied by their new dog, clattered down the back steps with merry shouts. It was a lovely, sunshiny day and there was much to make the children happy. They had a new trick dog, for one thing. Then they thought of the fun they would have when they got Snap and Snoop back. Besides, there was also the circus of which to think.

"I hope we can go to it!" murmured Bert.

"Oh, I think Mother will let us," said Nan.

"I guess Waggo is better than any trick dog they have in this circus!" boasted Freddie.

"Maybe they haven't any dogs," ventured Flossie.

"Oh, all circuses have trick dogs, don't they, Bert?" Freddie asked.

"Most of 'em do, I guess," answered the older Bobbsey boy. "But I don't believe this is much of a circus. If it were, it would have had the posters up all over town long ago."

"But they had an accident," Freddie said. "Flossie and I heard the men talking about it."

"Maybe," admitted Bert. "But I'd have to look this circus over before I could tell if it's a good one or not."

"Say, I know what let's do!" cried Nan with a sudden thought.

"What?" asked Bert.

"Let's all go down to the circus grounds and watch 'em put up the tents. Then, if we see any of the owners, we can sort of ask if they want to buy a trick dog."

"We aren't going to sell him to the circus, that is, not until Mother asks Dad." Bert corrected her.

"That's so. Well, let's go to the circus grounds, anyhow."

"All right!" Bert agreed.

"May we come?" asked Flossie.

"I'm coming!" Freddie decided for himself. "I know where it is. But I'm not going to take Waggo," he added.

"Why not?" asked Nan with a smiling look at Bert.

"Some of the men might try to coax him away from me. Waggo is a valuable dog and I don't want to lose him."

"It would be better to leave him home," agreed Bert. "He might get lost, anyhow, even if nobody tried to take him, and he hasn't any collar that we could fasten a rope to. Leave him home."

"Besides," suggested Flossie, "an elephant might step on him."

"We didn't see any elephants when we came past the circus grounds a little while ago," Freddie said.

"It would be a pretty poor circus without

elephants," declared Bert. "Come on we'll shut Waggo down cellar and go to the circus grounds."

"We'd better ask Mother first," suggested Nan.

"Yes, I guess we'd better," Bert agreed.

Mrs. Bobbsey gave permission, first making Nan and Bert promise to keep watch over Flossie and Freddie. Then the twins started forth, leaving behind them a sorrowful and whining Waggo, locked in the cellar.

"It's better for him to howl a little than be stepped on by an elephant," said Flossie.

Running along, the Bobbsey twins soon approached the circus grounds with its many wonderful sights.

CHAPTER IV

THE BIG TENT

"HELLO, Charlie!" called Bert Bobbsey as he saw one of his chums hurrying across the circus grounds.

"Oh, hello!" echoed Charlie. "Say, this is great, isn't it, the circus coming to town!"

"Wonderful!" agreed Bert.

"I didn't know it was coming," went on Charlie. "I didn't see any posters around town, or anything."

"Neither did I," admitted Bert. "Flossie and Freddie were the first to discover that the show was here. They came across the lots with their trick dog and saw the men putting up the tent. The circus had an accident, so the twins heard, and didn't plan to come here until later, but it had to."

"I'm glad it did," Charlie said. "Maybe we can get jobs carrying water for the elephants. But what's this about a trick dog?"

"It's a dog that came to us," Flossie was

quick to explain, "and he's half mine and half Freddie's and he does tricks and maybe we're going to sell him to a circus man and get a lot of money, and maybe we're going to keep him and get up a circus of our own, only we didn't bring our dog with us now because he might get stepped on by one of the elephants, though I don't see any." After this long sentence Flossie paused to get her breath and look over the circus grounds, where there were now many men and boys, horses and wagons.

"Oh, so that's how it happened!" remarked Charlie. Then he laughed and Bert laughed and Charlie exclaimed, "There's John Marsh. Come on, let's see if we can get jobs watering the elephants and maybe they'll give us free tickets."

"I suppose you think," said Nan with a little smile, "that the elephants carry circus tickets in their trunks."

"Oh, I mean the circus men may give us tickets!" Charlie corrected himself. "You caught me that time, Nan."

"But look!" Freddie suddenly exclaimed, "the big tent has fallen down. It's all over the grass. I guess there isn't going to be any circus!"

"Oh, dear! That's too bad!" sighed Flossie.

The children looked toward the middle of the circus grounds. Sure enough, covering a large part of the grass was a big piece of canvas about which were gathered many men, some with stakes, others with long poles and some with big hammers.

"The tent's fallen down!" said Freddie again.

"No, it hasn't," Bert told his brother and little sister. "They always have to lay the canvas of the big tent out flat on the ground like that before they hoist it up on poles."

"Oh, yes," Freddie said as he saw the men lacing together different sections of the "big top," as the circus main tent is called.

"Then is it all right?" Flossie wanted to know.

"Yes, dear, it's all right," Nan told her. "They'll have the tent up after a while. You see, it's so big they can't put it all up at once as Daddy did our small tent when we went camping."

"Oh, I'm glad there's going to be a circus," Flossie said, "'cause maybe our dog Waggo will do some tricks in it."

"I wonder if they have any fire engines here?" murmured Freddie. "I wish I could see a circus fire engine."

"They don't have fire engines in a circus," Flossie declared. "What is there to burn that they'd need an engine for?"

"The tent might catch fire," Freddie said. "I'm going to look for the fire engine. I want to see how it pumps."

Just then John Marsh who, with Charlie Mason, often played with Bert Bobbsey, came running toward the two boys.

"Isn't this fine!" cried John. "I didn't know they were going to have a circus here."

"Nobody else did either, I guess," Bert answered.

"Except your little brother and sister," corrected Charlie. "They are clever with their trick dog. But say, let's go see about watering the elephants."

Bert looked at Nan. She knew what he wanted to say. Bert had promised his mother to help look after Flossie and Freddie. But if he remained with the small twins there would be no chance to wander about with his chums as he pleased or to see about watering the big elephants, none of which was yet to be seen, however. So Nan kindly said:

"You may go with John and Charlie if you like, Bert."

"But what about them?" Bert nodded toward Flossie and Freddie, who were eagerly watching the men hauling on ropes that soon would raise the big tent on its supporting poles.

"I'll look after them," Nan agreed.

"Sure you don't mind?" Bert asked. He did not want to be selfish.

"No, I don't mind. I'll have fun with them. When they get tired I'll take them home and you needn't bother about them."

"Oh, all right! That's fine! Thanks!" Bert exclaimed as he ran off with his two chums.

"I'm not going to get tired!" declared Freddie, having heard what Nan said.

"I'm not, either! I'm not going home!" announced Flossie. "I want to stay and see all the circus and ask a man if he wants to buy our trick dog."

"Better not do that," advised Nan. "Let's wait and see what Daddy says about the dog. Maybe he belongs to someone around Lakeport and you'd have to give him up. Or if he doesn't, and we can keep him, it might be much nicer to save Waggo for ourselves. Since Snap went away we haven't had a dog."

"Maybe Snap will come back," remarked Flossie. "I wish he would."

"So do I, but I guess he's dead," said Freddie. "Or else he's gone far away and somebody is keeping him like we are keeping Waggo."

'I wish our cat Snoop would come back," spoke Flossie. "Of course, our Christmas cat is nice, but I like Snoop better."

"So did I," agreed her twin brother. "But come on, Nan. Take us closer so we can see 'em put up the tent better."

Seeing a clear place, where there was no crowd of working circus men, Nan led the little twins nearer to where the big tent was going up. She looked across the lots and saw her brother, together with Charlie and John, hurrying toward a smaller tent which had just been erected.

"That's the animal tent," said Nan to herself. "I guess they'll be putting the elephants in there pretty soon and the cages of lions and tigers."

As Nan came to a halt as near the big tent as she thought it safe to take her small charges, she heard the rumble of several heavy circus vans, each one drawn by four or more horses. Looking across the field she saw these big wagons advancing. Some of them had iron bars on each side, but there was either a canvas or a wooden screen about the bars so that whatever was inside could not be seen. As soon as Flossie and Freddie saw these vans they cried out:

"There go the animals!"

"Yes," Nan agreed, "those are the animal cages."

"Let's go over closer!" begged Freddie. "I want to see the lion."

"I'd rather see an elephant, though I haven't any peanuts to give him," Flossie remarked.

Nan saw a big crowd of boys and men now gathering about the rumbling animal cages which were being drawn toward the smaller tent. She did not think it would be wise to take Flossie and Freddie into that pushing, crowding throng. But the small twins begged to go.

"We want to see the animals!" insisted Freddie.

"You can't see anything," Nan answered. "The cages are closed now. I guess the animals are asleep."

"Maybe some of 'em are awake," suggested Flossie hopefully.

"Come on!" teased Freddie, pulling hard at Nan's hand.

Just then, from one of the covered cages, came a deep, rumbling roar. Both the small twins jumped back.

"That—that was a lion!" whispered Freddie.

"Yes, it sounded like a lion," agreed Nan.

"I guess maybe we'd better not go look at him now," whispered Flossie, as she pulled Nan the other way. "I think the lion just woke up and maybe he's cross. We'll wait until he gets inside the tent and then we'll see him after he feels better."

"Well—all right," Freddie said as more

and louder roars came from the wheeled cage. Then it suddenly tilted to one side and the men and boys in the crowd about it began to run away.

"Maybe the lion is going to break out!" suggested Freddie. and his voice was the least bit hopeful.

"I guess that's what he's trying to do," Nan said. "That's why the crowd is getting out of the way." She was glad she had not taken the twins into that throng. "But the cage is strong and the circus men won't let the lion get out," she added as she felt Flossie's fingers clasping her hand tighter. "There's nothing to be afraid of."

"Sure not!" agreed Freddie. "Anyhow, if the lion did get out maybe I could find the circus fire engine and squirt water on him. That's the way to make a lion run away from you—just squirt water on him."

"Let's go look for an elephant," suggested Flossie, still pulling Nan away from that part of the grounds where the animal tent was being put up.

"We'll see if we can find one," Nan agreed.

By this time the big tent was partly erected

and scores of men were hauling on long ropes that hoisted the big spread of canvas higher and higher on the supporting poles. Other men were putting gay flags and banners on poles and ropes so that in the sunshine the circus grounds were taking on a gay appearance.

Flossie and Freddie were having a fine time with Nan, watching all that went on. But look as they did, they could see no elephants. Nan knew, from having seen other circuses, that these big animals were never brought to the grounds in cages. They had to walk along in the open and so were a sort of free show.

"Where are the elephants?" demanded Freddie and, more than once, as Nan wandered about the grounds, Flossie asked the same question.

"I don't know where the elephants are," Nan said. "Maybe they haven't any."

"Then it isn't a regular circus!" declared Freddie as if that settled the matter.

Just then Nan saw a man who appeared to be one of the owners or managers of the show and she ventured to ask:

"Haven't you any elephants?"

"Oh, yes, plenty of elephants," he replied with a smile. "But everything is all mixed up. We had a delay and some accidents, nothing serious, but it has upset our plans. The elephants are still in the railroad cars. They'll be taken out tomorrow, so we aren't going to open until then and we'll be here several days. Oh, you'll see plenty of elephants," he went on, patting Flossie's yellow hair. "And big ones, too!"

"That's good!" said Freddie. "And have you a fire engine?"

"A fire engine!" repeated the circus man in some surprise.

"Oh, he's crazy about fire engines," said Nan with a laugh. "I guess he's going to be a fireman when he grows up."

"I see," said the man. "Well, yes, we have a sort of fire engine or pump, that we carry with us. But I hope we don't have to use it," he added. "It's no fun to have a circus catch fire."

"I shouldn't think so," agreed Nan as the man left them. Then she led the children farther about the grounds, letting them stop near the place where the side-show tent was being erected. In front of this were gay banners showing a woman holding up a number of snakes; one of another woman almost as fat as a baby elephant, and a picture of a man so thin that many of his bones showed.

"He's the living skelington," declared Freddie, pointing. "I'm going to see him."

"I'd rather see the big fat lady," Flossie said. "She looks so nice and laughing."

"You used to be quite fat yourself," remarked Nan. "Daddy called you his little fat fairy."

"Oh, I remember that!" cried Freddie. "Flossie was awful fat." Then, as he saw a man come out of a little tent with a dog, the small boy cried, "Let's go see him. Maybe that dog does tricks!"

As Flossie and Freddie, pulling hard at Nan's hands, reached the small tent behind which the man and the dog had taken their places, they saw the dog suddenly tilt himself up and walk on his front paws.

"Just like Waggo!" murmured Flossie.

"He's a trick circus dog just like ours!" exclaimed Freddie. "I'm going to talk to that man."

Before Nan could stop him, Freddie broke away from her and ran forward. She followed with Flossie in time to hear Freddie ask:

"Have you any more trick dogs?"

"Yes, I've half a dozen more," the man said. "This is a new dog and I have to make him practice more than I do my old ones. I lost a fine trick dog the other day. I wish I could get him back. He could walk on his hind legs and front legs, but best of all, he could beat a drum with his tail. I'd like to get that dog back!"

"Oh!" gasped Flossie.

"Oh!" murmured Freddie.

Then the small twins looked up at their sister Nan.

CHAPTER V

RETURNED WANDERERS

"Come on now, Pinto!" called the circus man to his trick dog. He did not seem to notice the alarmed looks on the faces of Flossie and Freddie. "Up on your hind legs, Pinto! That's right! Now on your front legs! Good! You're doing nicely. Now for the hard part! Over you go! Somersault! Turn!"

At this command the dog, which was of the poodle variety, ran a little way on the ground and then suddenly leaped into the air, turning a backward somersault as nicely as you please.

"Oh, that's wonderful!" murmured Flossie.

"A dandy trick!" echoed Freddie. "Our dog can't do that—anyhow, we've never tried to make him do it."

"Have you a trick dog?" asked the man suddenly, pausing as he patted his own animal gently on the head, and giving him a bit of sweet cracker as a reward for doing the somersault trick. "Did you say you had a trick dog?"

He looked sharply at Flossie, then at Freddie and finally at Nan. In their imaginations the small twins saw their lovely air castles tumbling down. They felt sure that the dog which had come to them was the one that had escaped from the circus. They felt that Waggo, as they had named him, belonged to this man and that he would claim the dog they loved. They could not have him in their own little circus if they got one up, nor could they sell him and get some money as Freddie had hoped. It was too bad.

Then Freddie told himself, "Maybe this man will give us a reward for keeping Waggo, or whatever his name is."

Before either Flossie or Freddie could answer the circus man's question, Nan broke in to inquire:

"What kind of a dog was the one you lost, I mean your trick dog?"

She hoped he would say a poodle, like the one that had just turned a somersault. But the man replied:

"My dog was a sort of fox-terrier, but he had a long tail instead of a short one as most terriers have. That's how he could beat a drum with his tail. A terrier with a little stump of a tail couldn't very well beat a drum, could he?"

"No," answered Freddie, and his heart was sad as he thought of how Waggo with his long tail had drummed a tattoo on Dinah's dishpan. Surely the stray terrier must belong to this circus man.

"What was your dog's name?" asked Nan, knowing just how bad the small twins felt.

"His name was Skippo," the man answered. "Besides doing the tricks of standing on his hind and front paws, playing dead, beating a drum and turning somersaults, Skippo could jump rope as well as a girl. That's why I called him Skippo."

"Our trick dog can't jump rope," murmured Flossie. "Anyhow, we haven't tried him at that yet."

"What kind of a trick dog have you and where did you get him?" asked the man as he got ready to have his pet perform again for practice. "Where did you get him?"

Freddie was about to say that the dog had wandered into the yard at home when Nan interposed again to ask:

"Did your trick dog run away from you?"

"Oh, no," replied the circus man. "He died. He got sick, couldn't do his tricks and then, all of a sudden, he up and died on me."

"Oh, that's too bad," murmured Nan, though she could not help feeling glad that the dog Flossie and Freddie had could not, by any possibility, belong to this man, whose missing dog was dead.

"I'm sorry!" said Flossie.

"So am I!" chimed in Freddie. "I'm glad our trick dog isn't dead, though. But he can't turn a somersault like yours can."

"We didn't ask him to," said Flossie.

"No," Freddie agreed, "we didn't ask him. But we will when we go back home," he added.

"Tell me more about your dog," begged the circus man. "Since mine died, I'm short one animal in my final act in the side show, and I need a new dog. If yours is any good I might buy him."

This was just what Freddie had been

thinking of all along, and now, at the mention of it, his eyes sparkled. Nan was more careful about it as she said:

"We aren't sure we can sell this dog, or even that we want to. Our father will have to be told about it."

"Well, little girl, tell your father that Jim Hatton, or Professor Mungo, as they call me, who has an animal act in the Selby Brothers' Circus, wants to buy a good trick dog and he'll pay well. I don't want to take advantage of you children, but I'd like a dog in the place of mine that died. Come and see me again. Now then, Pinto, up with you!"

He began to put his dog through some new tricks. Flossie and Freddie looked on with eager eyes, but Nan was bent upon getting away. She feared that the small twins might offer to sell Waggo on their own responsibility. They might even slip away from her, get the dog and bring him to the circus grounds, turning him over to Jim Hatton, or Professor Mungo, which was the man's circus name. She was wondering what to do, for it seemed hard to get Flossie and Freddie away from watching Pinto practice his tricks, when suddenly on the other side of the circus lot a cry arose:

"Here come the elephants!"

"Oh, the elephants!" gasped Flossie. "The elephants!"

"Let's go see 'em!" begged Freddie, turning away from Profesor Mungo and his performing dog. "Hurry! I want to see the elephants!"

"We haven't any peanuts for them," sighed Flossie. "But maybe, on the way over," she added as she started across the lot with Nan and Freddie, "maybe we can see a man selling some. I have five cents!"

"I'll buy the peanuts for you," kindly offered her brother. "Give me the nickel."

"No, I'll buy them myself," declared Flossie, her hand thrust deep into the little pocket of her dress.

"Oh, look! There are the elephants!" cried Freddie, all excited. "Wow! Look!"

"Big ones, too!" added Flossie. "Oh! Oh!"

"And I see Bert, Charlie and John following them," said Nan as she caught sight of her brother with several other boys in the crowd around the large, shuffling animals.

"I wonder if Bert carried any water for the elephants?" said Freddie. "I'd like to do that."

"Maybe they haven't watered them yet," Nan suggested. "We'll go closer and have a look before they put them in the tent," for the elephants were being led toward the animal tent.

Flossie and Freddie were delighted, as were many other children, by a free view of the big elephants with the Selby circus, of which there was a herd of ten. The animals had just been taken from their cages in railroad cars and were being hurried toward the grounds. The circus train was on the railroad siding not far from the big field where the show was to be held for several days.

"Hello, Bert!" Nan called as her brother ran past her in the crowd with his two chums. "Have you watered the elephants yet?"

"No, not yet. They won't hold still long enough. But when they get in the tent maybe we can carry water for 'em and get a free ticket."

"We're all going to get free tickets!" said John Marsh.

"I wish I could get a free ticket," sighed Flossie.

"Girls can't carry water for elephants," declared Freddie. "Only boys can do that. I'm going to help Bert," and he tried to draw away from Nan.

"No, you aren't!" she decided. "You're going to stay right here with me. The elephants are too big for you."

"May I give them some peanuts?" Flossie wanted to know.

"Perhaps after a while," Nan answered. "The circus hasn't opened yet. It probably won't be open until tomorrow on account of the mix-up and delay because of the accident, whatever it was. When we come to the circus, then you can buy some peanuts. It would be only a waste of time to try to give peanuts to elephants that are hurrying along as these are."

It was true, for the circus men were making the big animals fairly run toward their sheltering tent. An elephant is big and clumsy, but when he wants to run and hurry he can go pretty fast.

There was now such a large crowd about

the elephants that Nan was glad when she could lead her brother and sister away from it. The big animals were soon hidden inside their tent, and men on guard would not let any of the boys in—not even Bert, John or Charlie, who offered to carry pails of water from Lake Metoka, which was not far from the circus grounds.

With the elephants shut away from view, and the other animals in cages and also behind canvas walls, there was little of a free show to be seen now. Of course, there were busy scenes on the circus grounds. The big tent was still only partly up and men were working hard at erecting it. The kitchen and dining tents had been set up and from the former appetizing meals were coming. White-capped cooks were busy stirring large cauldrons of soup that were steaming over great iron stoves.

This smell of cooking reminded Nan, as well as Flossie and Freddie, that it was close to their own lunch hour. So, though the small twins begged to stay and see more, they were finally persuaded, by reason of their hunger, to move toward home.

"We can come again this afternoon," Nan said.

"And we'll come to the circus show tomorrow," declared Freddie.

"If Mother lets us," added Nan.

"Maybe we'll bring Waggo and let the trick dog man look at him," suggested Flossie.

"Daddy will have something to say about that," spoke Nan. "I am sure now, from having seen Pinto, that the dog which came to us is quite valuable. If we sell him, though I'm not sure we can, he ought to bring a lot of money."

"Then we'll be rich!" exclaimed Freddie joyfully.

"Oh, hardly that!" and Nan laughed. "Besides, the dog may belong to somebody else. We'll find out by advertising."

Even though they were hungry, Flossie and Freddie did not want to come away from the circus grounds. Nan had to fairly drag them with her and they kept turning about to see what was happening.

At last they were on the main streets of Lakeport and soon were hurrying in the direction of their home. The small twins were eagerly talking of what they had seen. Nan was wondering what was to be done about the trick dog.

Then suddenly, as the three turned into their side yard, they heard loud barking.

"That's Waggo!" exclaimed Freddie.

"But there's another dog!" cried Flossie. "There are two dogs!"

"Yes, there are!" agreed Nan. "I think I know that other dog's bark. I've heard it before many times."

"Who is it?" asked Freddie. "Is it Snap, do you think?"

Before Nan could answer there was a rush of feet around the corner of the house and soon a dog was leaping excitedly and joyously about the children, trying to lick their faces and hands with his red tongue.

"Oh, it's Snap!" cried Freddie. "It's our old dog Snap come back to us!"

"Yes, and here's Snoop, our old cat!" cried Flossie as she caught sight of the pussy slowly following Snap along the side path. "Oh, we have both our old pets back! Isn't it wonderful!"

"And a new one—for here's Waggo!" cried

Freddie as the trick dog also made his appearance.

"We've the beginning of a regular menagerie with two dogs, and Snoop, and the Christmas cat," chuckled Nan. "Oh, look out!" she cried as Snap suddenly turned around, showing his teeth and growling at Waggo. "Look out! They're going to fight!"

CHAPTER VI

A BATH TUB RESCUE

STANDING a little distance apart on the path at the side of the house, Snap, the old Bobbsey dog and Waggo, the new trick Bobbsey dog, looked at each other, growling and showing their teeth.

"Come on!" cried Nan to Flossie and Freddie, reaching out to take hold of their hands. "I must get you two safely into the house before they fight."

"They aren't going to fight!" declared Bert, who came along just then. "They're only growling and making believe. I guess Snap didn't like it when he got back after his wanderings and found the new dog here."

"I'm glad Snap is back," said Freddie.

"I'm glad Snoop is back," said Flossie, looking at the sleek old cat which had been away almost as long as had Snap. "Oh, look," went on the little girl, "Snoop and the Christmas cat are making friends."

This was true. The Christmas cat, which the Bobbsey twins had found in their cellar with her little family of kittens, was purring and rubbing up against Snoop, who in turn seemed very fond of his new acquaintance.

"If only the dogs would be friendly like that," murmured Nan, still keeping hold of Flossie and Freddie, for she feared they might go too close to the angry animals.

"I'll make 'em be friendly!" declared Bert, going toward Snap.

"Oh, be careful!" warned Nan.

"There's no danger, Snap won't nip me," went on Bert. "Here!' he ordered, "behave yourself and make friends with this new dog. Waggo, this is Snap," said the Bobbsey boy. "Snap, this is Waggo. He's a trick dog. See what he can do! Give us your paw, Waggo!"

Bert held out his hand and Waggo, sitting down on his hind legs, held out a front paw as if shaking hands.

"Now stand on your hind legs!" Bert ordered, and Waggo did that.

"Make him stand on his front legs and walk!" begged Flossie.

"Go ahead, do that!" Bert said, lifting

Waggo's hind paws a little way off the ground to show what trick he wanted the dog to do.

"If he could only turn a somersault he would be as good as the circus dog," murmured Freddie.

"Maybe he can," Bert said. "We'll try him on that after a while. What I want him to do now is to make friends with Snap. Look there, Snap," he went on, "this dog is smarter than you are, though you used to do tricks when you were younger. Aren't you ashamed of growling and barking at him? Shame on you! Be friends!"

Bert spoke rather crossly to Snap. Now, whether it was the tone of voice Bert used or because Snap was jealous that Waggo was more thought of by the children than he was, I cannot say.

Anyway, Snap drooped his tail between his legs as he always did when he knew he had done something wrong and had been scolded for it. He looked as if he were ashamed of himself. Then he gave a little whine, as if saying he was sorry, and walked up to Waggo.

"Be careful now!" warned Nan.

"Oh, nothing is going to happen except something good, I know," said Bert with a laugh.

Waggo watched Snap come closer to him. Up to this time neither dog had wagged his tail. Almost always it is a good sign when a dog wags his tail. When a dog does not wag his tail it often means that he is angry or afraid.

Now, all of a sudden, Waggo gave his dish-pan-drumming-tail a flip. First he wagged it only a little. Then he wagged it hard to and fro. Snap did the same thing, first shaking his tail only a little and then, as he watched the other dog, wagging it hard.

"Now they're all right," said Bert.

Truly they were, for, after touching noses ("kissing," Flossie called it) the two animals walked around each other, side by side, and finally they both lay down in the grass.

"Now they surely are friends!" said Freddie.

"That's right," agreed Bert. "There won't be any more trouble between them." There was not. "Only," went on Bert, "I wish Snap could do some tricks like Waggo."

"Maybe he learned some tricks while he was away," suggested Freddie. "We can try him. Perhaps when he sees Waggo doing circus tricks it will make Snap want to do them."

"Maybe," agreed Bert. "We'll see."

"Look at the cats!" laughed Flossie. "They made friends at once."

"So they did," agreed Nan. "Now we have a lot of animals," she went on, "two dogs and two cats and some kittens."

"It's nice!" Freddie declared.

"We can have a circus all our own," went on Flossie. "Only," she made haste to say, "I want to go to the regular circus just the same, and give the elephants some peanuts."

"So do I!" echoed Freddie.

For some time the Bobbsey twins stayed with their pets, talking to them and wondering where Snap and Snoop had been all these months.

"It's queer they came back at the same time," observed Nan.

"Isn't it!" said Bert. "If they could only talk they might tell us some strange adventures they had."

"Wouldn't it be fun if they could!" exclaimed Nan.

"It looks just as if Snoop and our Christmas cat were talking," said Flossie. "Look! They have their noses close together just like Uncle Dan's horses do at Meadow Brook."

"And the dogs are talking, too," spoke Freddie, as he saw Snap and Waggo with their heads close together.

"Maybe," said Bert with a laugh and a sly wink at Nan, "Waggo is telling Snap how to do circus tricks."

While the children were playing with their pets after luncheon, they were surprised to hear a voice asking:

"What's all this? Is this an animal show?"

"Oh, Daddy!" cried Flossie, springing up and running to greet her father, "we've such wonderful news!"

"What kind of news, little fat fairy?" Mr. Bobbsey asked, though Flossie was not now so little nor so fat as she had been when younger.

"The circus is here!" gasped Flossie, "and that new dog we have can do circus tricks, and Snap is back and so is Snoop."

"So I see," murmured Mr. Bobbsey, recognizing the old pets. "I thought they had run away forever or were both dead. I'm glad they're back. That's a lot of news."

"That isn't all!" Freddie made haste to say. "We're going to the circus and they have a fire engine squirter and if the elephants run away I'm going to squirt water on 'em— maybe," he added after a pause.

"Well, my little fireman, we'll see about that," Mr. Bobbsey said. "But what's this about a trick dog?"

Then the children told how, unexpectedly, they had discovered that Waggo could do several tricks. By turns Bert, Nan, Flossie and Freddie told all that had happened since morning when Mr. Bobbsey had gone to his office. It was now late afternoon and he had come home.

"Freddie wants to sell the trick dog to the circus man," explained Bert, "but I think it would be better to keep him. Only Mother says we can't do either until you think about it and maybe advertise to see who owns the trick dog."

"I think that must be done," Mr. Bobbsey agreed as his wife came out into the yard. "But let me see Waggo do some tricks," suggested the children's father suddenly.

"I'll make him do 'em!" cried Freddie. "I can do it best."

"I'll help," offered Flossie. "He's half my dog, anyhow."

Together the small twins made Waggo perform his tricks, which the dog seemed to do very willingly. He sat up, rolled over, walked on his hind and front legs and shook paws.

"Now I'll show you how he can drum," concluded Freddie. "I'll go get Dinah's dishpan."

"Better not," warned his mother with a laugh. "Dinah is getting supper ready and she won't want to be bothered with a boy or a dog."

"But I must have something for a drum to show how Waggo bangs it," went on Freddie.

"Here, use this box," suggested Bert, bringing over a small one. When it was set on end, just as the dishpan was, Waggo thumped his tail against the wooden bottom, making a sound quite as if he were banging on a drum.

"A very clever dog," said Mr. Bobbsey.

"You ought to see him kiss Dinah!"

"He's worth a lot of money, isn't he, Daddy?" asked Freddie.

"Yes, I think he may be," Mr. Bobbsey agreed.

"But do you think he should be sold to a circus?" asked Nan.

"Wouldn't it be better for us to keep him and make up our own circus, now that we have Snap and Snoop back?" Bert wanted to know.

"My! Such a lot of questions!" said Mrs. Bobbsey, smiling. "I don't see how Daddy can answer them all. But I must ask one myself," she went on. "Don't you think, Richard," she said to her husband, "that this dog should be advertised in the paper so if the owner lives around here he can claim him?"

"That would be the fair thing to do, first," Mr. Bobbsey said. "If you had lost this dog, I mean if he were really yours," he said to the children, "you would want whoever found him to give him back, wouldn't you?"

"Oh, sure!" Bert said.

"Then we must advertise."

"Well, I hope nobody claims him," sighed Nan.

"So do I!" said Flossie and Freddie together as if they were practicing a duet.

Bert went over to Snap and talked to his old pet. This the dog seemed to like. He may have thought, with Waggo getting so much attention on account of his clever tricks, that poor old Snap was not wanted any more.

"But I like you!" whispered Bert, and Snap wagged his tail happily.

The next day Mr. Bobbsey put an advertisement in the *Lakeport Times* stating that a trick dog had come to the Bobbsey home and that its owner could have him by calling and proving his property.

"What does that mean, 'proving his property'?" asked Freddie as he read the note in the paper.

"It means," Bert explained, "that whoever comes must show that he knows Waggo, by whatever his name was before we named him, and he has to make him do some tricks, maybe tricks that we haven't made him do, for we don't know all that he can do."

"Oh," said Freddie, "I see. Well, I hope nobody comes for him."

"So do I!" sighed Flossie.

The next two days were ones of anxious waiting. Several times the Bobbsey twins went to the circus grounds, but the show was not yet ready to open, for some of the animals and much of the material had not as yet arrived. There had been a railroad accident before the show finally changed plans and came unexpectedly to Lakeport. But now there were many posters on walls and fences of the town stating that the show would open soon and remain there for several days.

"We'll all go!" declared Bert when he came home one afternoon with his sisters and brothers, having gone to the grounds to get a glimpse of anything that might be seen. Most of the animals were in the closed tents, however, though now and then an elephant could be observed sticking out a waving trunk.

"Did anybody come for Waggo while we were at the circus?" asked Nan of her mother, for the two dogs had been left at home when the children went sight-seeing.

"Yes," said Mrs. Bobbsey, "a man called."

"Did he take Waggo?" cried all the twins at once.

"No," was the reply, and they were all happy again. "His dog wasn't this kind. He didn't know Waggo and Waggo didn't know him."

"Oh, I'm glad!" cried Nan, and so were her brothers and sister.

It was two days after this, and nearly time for the circus show to open, that Flossie, who was up in the bathroom brushing her teeth, suddenly gave a loud cry.

"Oh! Oh!" shouted the little girl. "She's fallen in!"

"Oh, Flossie must be in the bath tub! It's full of water where I was soaking some new sheets and pillow cases!" exclaimed Mrs. Bobbsey. "Quick, Bert! Nan! Get Flossie out!"

Bert ran up the stairs, three steps at a jump, toward the bathroom whence came Flossie's cries. Mingled with them was the barking of Waggo, the trick dog.

CHAPTER VII

TO THE CIRCUS

"Flossie! Flossie! Are you all right?" cried her mother as she hurried into the bathroom after Bert. Nan followed. Freddie was out on the porch playing with his toy fire engine which, he said, "squirted real water," so he was not present at the rescue.

Somewhat to the surprise of Bert and his mother, Flossie answered plainly:

"Yes. I'm all right!"

"Then what's the matter?" asked Bert, who was now at the door. "It doesn't sound as if she had fallen in. She doesn't talk blub-bery-ubbery, like anyone does who's in the water."

Then the little girl called again:

"Oh, she's in the water just the same, but Waggo is getting her out! Good dog, Waggo!"

Much puzzled, Bert pushed open the bathroom door and there he saw a queer sight.

Flossie was quite all right, standing near

the wash-basin with her toothbrush in her hand. But floundering in the bath tub, which was filled with water nearly to the brim, was Waggo swimming about, and in his mouth was one of Flossie's dolls.

"Why," exclaimed Bert with a laugh when he saw that his sister was safe, "Waggo is a regular rescue dog! He's rescuing Flossie's doll!"

"Well, I'm glad it was the *doll* in the bath tub and not *Flossie*," said Mrs. Bobbsey. "How did your doll fall in?"

"She didn't *fall* in," was the answer as Waggo, swimming to the side of the tub, held himself partly out of the water by putting two paws over the edge while he stretched out his neck, with the doll in his mouth, toward Bert.

"Well, how'd she get in if she didn't fall in?" Mrs. Bobbsey asked.

"Waggo *put* her in," said Flossie.

"You mean the dog dropped your doll in the tub of water?" Nan inquired.

"Yes, he did," Flossie said with such a hard shake of her head that some of the tooth-paste foam was scattered on the towel she had draped in front of her to protect her dress.

"You see," went on the little girl, "I brought my dolly up here so I could have her brush her teeth when I brushed mine. She's just learning how to brush her teeth," she went on.

"Silly!" murmured Bert. "As if a doll could brush her own teeth."

"Of *course* she can when I show her *how!*" exclaimed Flossie with a sharp look at her brother.

"Pooh!" went on Bert. "Anyhow," he said with a laugh, "a doll's teeth don't need brushing. They're made of china or something like that."

"My doll's teeth are *real* and they need brushing same as mine do," declared Flossie with dignity.

"Ha! Ha!" chuckled Bert.

"Don't," warned his mother in a whisper. "Let Flossie alone. Go on, my dear," she said.

"Well, anyhow," resumed the little girl, "I brought my dolly up here to brush her teeth," and she looked sharply at Bert. "I was brushing my teeth first, so she would know how when, all of a sudden, up came Waggo. My doily was sitting on a chair. But he picked her up in his mouth, before I could stop him, and dropped her into the tub of water. Then he jumped in himself and got her out."

"Why, he's a regular rescue dog!" cried Bert admiringly as he took the doll from Waggo's mouth.

"Look out! Don't let him shake himself and scatter water all over!" cried Mrs. Bobbsey as Waggo scrambled out of the tub. She knew how dogs shake themselves after getting wet. She had seen Snap do it more than once.

"Here! I'll put this big bath mat over him!" exclaimed Nan, taking it from the rack. "That will partly dry him off."

In a moment Waggo was well covered and he seemed to enjoy being rubbed dry by Nan. Flossie took up her wet doll and said:

"Oh, dear!"

"Never mind," consoled her mother, "you can hang her clothes out on the line and dry them."

Then Bert had an idea.

"Do you know," he said to Nan, who now

took the bath mat off Waggo, "I believe this is a trick."

"What trick?" asked Nan.

"This rescue business. I mean, it's a trick Waggo has been used to doing and if we can make him do it regularly it will be something else for our circus when we get it up."

"Oh, wouldn't it!" agreed Nan eagerly. "But maybe it was an accident. I mean, it just might have happened that Waggo knocked the doll in by accident. Lots of dogs will get sticks or other things they see in the water."

"My doll didn't fall in by accident!" objected Flossie. "Waggo dropped her in the bath tub himself. I saw him."

"Well, we can soon tell," decided Bert. "Here, let me take the doll," he said to Flossie, reaching for it.

"What are you going to do?" demanded the little girl, clasping her "child" in her arms. Some of the doll's wet clothes had been taken off for drying.

"I want to put the doll on a chair and see if Waggo will drop her in again and rescue her," Bert answered.

"No! No!" cried Flossie, backing away. "You aren't going to play any tricks with my doll! She was 'most drowned once and I'm not going to have her wet again."

"Well, then, let me take an old doll," begged Bert.

"Yes, do, Flossie," suggested Nan, who felt herself rather too old, now, to play with dolls. "Let him take that old rubber doll I gave you last year. It won't hurt her to get wet."

Nan was as much interested as was Bert in seeing if this rescue were really a trick on the part of Waggo or just a chance happening. Waggo stood in the middle of the bathroom, partly dry now. He was looking from one to the other of the children, his bright eyes seeming to snap, while his head was cocked on one side as if he wanted to ask what they thought of it all.

"All right," Flossie said after a while, "I'll get you my old rubber doll, Bert. But first I must finish brushing my teeth and then my dolly has to brush hers."

"I should think the doll's teeth would be clean now after her swim," said Bert with a laugh.

"Well, yes, maybe," Flossie agreed after thinking it over. "Yes, I guess they're clean enough," she admitted, taking a look as she murmured, "Oh, you poor, dear child!" Then she said, "But I have to brush my own teeth."

"Hurry up!" begged Bert. "I want to see if Waggo can do this trick."

When the rubber doll was brought up and put on a chair, the dog suddenly seized it, dropped it into the tub and then jumped in to the rescue as he had done the other time.

"It's a trick! It's a trick!" cried Bert in delight.

"It surely is!" agreed Nan. "What a smart dog!"

"Are you going to have him do that trick in a circus?" asked Flossie.

"Yes, I guess so," Bert assented. "But I'll try him a couple of more times."

This he did, and Waggo never once made a mistake. He made several "rescues," much to the delight of the children. Freddie, hearing the laughter up in the bathroom, left his fire engine toy and came up to see what was happening.

"I told you he was a smart dog!"

"Yes, he is," Bert agreed. "We'll have a lot of fun with him. This rescue act will be a good one. If he were a bigger dog he could rescue a real child instead of a doll."

"I believe he could," said Nan.

Mr. Bobbsey was told about the new trick Waggo had done, and patted the dog. He also patted old Snap, not wanting that animal to feel sad at being neglected.

"Do you think anybody will claim this dog now?" asked Bert, twiddling Waggo's ears.

"No," his father answered, "I hardly think so now. The advertisement has been in nearly a week, and though several persons have called to see about it, none of them could prove that they owned Waggo. I guess you may keep the dog."

"Oh, goodie!" cried Flossie and Freddie, and Bert and Nan smiled their delight.

"May we go to the circus when it opens?" asked Bert.

"Yes, I guess so," his father said. "When does it start?"

"Tomorrow!" cried all the Bobbsey twins together, for they had carefully noted the date on the posters about town.

"Then I'll declare a holiday and we'll all go to the circus," said Mr. Bobbsey.

"But we won't take Waggo or Snap or the cats," Flossie said. "Some of the circus men might want them."

"Or an elephant might step on them," added Freddie.

"Yes, it will be better to leave the pets at home," Mrs. Bobbsey said. "I hope tomorrow will be a nice day."

The children also hoped this and the hope came true; it was as fine a day as heart could wish. Bright and early the Bobbsey twins were awake and after breakfast they got ready to go downtown and watch the circus parade.

"Oh, won't we have fun!" murmured Flossie as they started on their way.

"Piles of fun!" echoed Freddie. "Hurray! Hurray!"

CHAPTER VIII

A RUNAWAY ELEPHANT

HURRYING along, pushing to and fro, running here and there, shouting, laughing and squealing with delight, the boys and girls of Lakeport, with many of their fathers, mothers, uncles, aunts, grandfathers and grandmothers were hastening downtown to watch the circus parade along Main Street. In the throng, happiest of all, were the Bobbsey twins. Flossie and Freddie walked in front, with their parents just behind them. Nan was nearby with Nellie Parks, Grace Lavine and Helen Porter, her best chums. Bert had with him Charlie Mason and John Marsh.

"Here's a good place!" exclaimed Nan as the little party reached an open space along the sidewalk. "We can see the circus fine from here, Mother."

"Yes, it is a good place," agreed Mrs. Bobbsey. "There's an old carriage stepping-stone for Flossie and Freddie to stand on so they can look over the heads of the people who get in front of them."

Years ago, in Lakeport, many families, including the Bobbseys, had horses and carriages instead of autos. In the early days there was placed at the street curb, in front of most houses, a block of stone so the ladies could more easily get into the carriages. It was one of these old stepping-stones that Mrs. Bobbsey pointed out as a good place for the small twins to stand.

"Oh, this'll be dandy!" cried Freddie when he saw it. "Come on, Flossie. This is great!"

Freddie jumped up onto the stone, while Bert and Nan, with their father and mother and the children's chums, took their places back of the old block. But, to the surprise of all, Flossie did not get up beside her little brother.

"What's the matter, Flossie?" asked Bert. "Don't you want to see the circus parade?"

"Of course I do," answered the little girl.

"Then why don't you get up on the stone beside Freddie?" Nan wanted to know.

"I think Freddie ought to have helped me up on the stone before he got up himself," said Flossie with dignity. "I saw a picture of some ladies getting into a carriage, off a stone just like this, and a gentleman was helping them step up. I think Freddie ought to have helped me instead of jumping up first himself."

"Well, what do you know about that!" exclaimed Bert with a laugh in which his chums joined.

"Flossie is right!" said her mother. "Boys and gentlemen should always help girls and ladies first. Freddie!" she called.

"Yes, Mother. What is it?" he asked, not turning around. "If you please, I can't come now, for I'm looking down the street to see if the circus is coming."

"Oh, I'm not going to take you away," his mother said with a laugh. "But look at Flossie."

"What's the matter with her?" Freddie wanted to know. "Is she lost again?"

Getting lost was one of the things Flossie could do best, as both her brothers well knew.

"No, she isn't lost," Mrs. Bobbsey said. "But can't you help her up onto the stone beside you?"

"Sure I can!" Freddie answered. "But what's the matter. Has she hurt her leg?"

"No, I haven't hurt my leg!" exclaimed Flossie. "My legs are as good as yours, Freddie Bobbsey. But I should think you might be polite and help me up, instead of getting up first yourself."

"There's an answer for you!" murmured Bert to John.

Freddie looked puzzled a moment, then as he smiled he said:

"Oh, excuse me! I forgot." Assuming an air of old-fashioned dignity, and acting as he had once acted in a school play, Freddie stepped off the stone, made a low bow to his little sister and then helped her to step upon the carriage stone.

"That's my little fireman!" said Mr. Bobbsey. "Are you all right now, my little fat fairy?" he asked.

"Yes, Daddy, I'm all right," was the answer. Then to her brother Flossie made a little bow and said, "Thank you, Mr. Freddie."

"You are quite welcome, Miss Flossie," he answered. Then they both laughed and Bert asked his little brother and sister:

"Is the circus coming?"

"I can't see it yet," Freddie answered.

Flossie exclaimed:

"I think I can hear the steam piano."

The children always called the Calliope by this name. You know this is pronounced Cal-*ly*-o-pee. It was more of a steam organ than a steam piano, but the name did not much matter. A circus parade would not be a circus parade without the Calliope, which was a big wagon carrying a steam boiler. Hot coals made steam in the boiler, and a man threw on fresh coal as it was needed. Back of the boiler sat another man at a keyboard something like that of a piano. Instead of wire strings, the Calliope had a number of metal pipes, like those in a church organ. As the man pressed the keys he sent jets of steam through these pipes and so played a tune. Always, long before you can see a circus parade, you can tell it is coming down the street by the loud music of the Calliope, or steam piano, as the Bobbsey children had called it.

"Yes, I hear it, too!" said Nan. "Oh, the parade is coming."

"Stand still now, children, and don't push

out into the street and get mixed up in the crowd," advised Mrs. Bobbsey as the throngs began to press closer around the little party of the twins and their friends. "Keep your places."

"We will," Nan promised.

"This is a dandy place to see the parade," remarked Charlie.

"Fine!" Bert answered.

"Let us all three go to the circus together," proposed John to Bert and Charlie, and they agreed to go down to the lot soon after dinner.

Louder and clearer sounded the music of the Calliope. Though it was at the very tail end of the parade, the wind was blowing away from it and so carried the gay tunes to the ears of the children.

The crowds in the street, and around the place which the Bobbseys had picked out as a vantage point, began to surge to and fro. Suddenly Flossie called:

"Mother, make Freddie stop!"

"What's he doing now?" asked Mrs. Bobbsey. She and her husband stood back of Bert, Nan and the other girls and boys, making a sort of guard about the stone on which the two small twins stood. "What's Freddie doing?"

"He's getting down off the stone and going out into the street," Flossie reported. "Maybe an elephant will step on him."

"Don't do that, Freddie," his mother cautioned.

"I'm not doing anything," he answered. "I just stepped off with one leg so I could look down the street and see better. I think I saw the horses," he said eagerly.

"Stay on the stone!" his father told him. "You'll be safer there."

"I'm getting back on," Freddie said. "Help pull me back, Flossie," he begged. "I saw the horses coming!" he fairly shouted. "Here comes the circus!"

Flossie obligingly helped her little brother back on the stone and now, from down the street, came the cries of:

"Here comes the parade!"

"Here it comes!"

"Oh, hear the music!"

There was a band, as well as the steam

piano, and from the top of a high wagon, gay with red paint, gilding and mirrors glistening in the sun, the musicians in scarlet coats blared out jolly tunes.

Following the joyful cries that told of the coming of the first part of the parade, there was a silence; but a moment later could be heard the clatter of the iron shoes of many horses on the pavement.

"Look! Look!" cried the children.

Down the street came the circus parade. Slowly the leading horses came opposite the Bobbsey twins. The band wagon led the procession, and behind it was another van, like it, filled with clowns dressed in gay suits, their faces daubed with red, blue, green and yellow paint. Some of the clowns were pretending to play big tin horns, making strange music. Others were beating drums and one clown was hitting another over the head with a rubber football.

"Oh, aren't they funny!" murmured Flossie.

"They'll do a lot of funny tricks in the tent," Freddie said, as he fumbled in his pocket.

"What you got?" Flossie asked her brother, shifting about on the stepping-stone.

"Peanuts," he answered. "I got a bag full for the elephants and we'll feed 'em when we go to the circus. But we can eat a few ourselves now if you like."

"Oh—I like!" exclaimed Flossie with a laugh. "Please give me some, Freddie."

So the two little twins munched peanuts as they watched the circus parade rumble past.

"Look at the lions!" called Bert as a cage of these savage beasts passed.

"And the hippopotamus!" added John. "Isn't he big!"

"But look at that cage of tigers!" cried Charlie, pointing to the next wagon. "There's a man sitting in with 'em and he hasn't any gun! Say, if those tigers went for him——"

"Aw, but he has a big whip," Bert said. "Tigers in a cage are more afraid of a whip than they are of a gun, I guess."

"Maybe he has a gun where you can't see it," suggested Charlie.

"Maybe," John agreed.

"Anyhow, I wouldn't want to be in the cage

with those tigers even if I had a gun," said Bert, and the other boys agreed with him.

There were more cages of animals; then came a herd of camels with men dressed like the Arabs of the desert sitting between the two humps. Suddenly was heard the always thrilling cry of:

"Here come the elephants!"

Swinging slowly into view came a herd of the big beasts. Amid the silence the shuffle of their padded feet could be heard on the pavement. Flossie and Freddie held their breaths in delighted wonder as they ate peanuts, scarcely taking time to remove the shells. The peanuts were good, brown and freshly roasted. Freddie had bought them on the way to see the parade.

Suddenly, as one of the largest elephants came opposite the Bobbsey twins, there was a commotion in the herd. A man's voice cried out excitedly. At once more of the elephant keepers shouted. Then without warning, a great beast broke out of the line of march and made a runaway dash straight for the Bobbsey twins!

CHAPTER IX

THE DOG SHOW

"Look out!" cried Mrs. Bobbsey.

"Run this way!" advised Mr. Bobbsey.

He and his wife each made a grab, one for Flossie and the other for Freddie. Bert and Nan, their parents felt, could get out of the way in time—out of the way of the charging elephant that was shuffling along on his feet, which were almost as large as butter tubs, straight toward the children.

There was a wild commotion in the crowd. Several of the circus men, who had been walking beside the herd of elephants in the parade, shouted to the other keepers to get the beasts back in line. For when the one big animal had stepped out of the ranks and made a dash for the Bobbsey twins, some of its companions had acted as though they, too, wanted to get away.

"Get back there, Princess! Steady, Major! Hold on there, Rajah!"

"Oh, Bert! What's going to happen?" cried Nan as her brother, pushing her in front of him, sought a place of safety.

"It'll be all right!" he answered. "They'll catch that elephant before he goes very far."

"Is he coming after us?" asked Nan with a frightened look over her shoulder.

"He's coming," Bert reported, as he, also, took a look. "But I don't believe he's coming for us."

"Why, Bert Bobbsey! He's headed right this way!" screamed Nan.

"Yes, but I guess he just wants to get away —to be free. Maybe he's tired of being in a circus," Bert said as he hastened along with Nan, following others in the throng who were, likewise, seeking a way of escape. "I don't believe he specially wants us," Bert said.

"Well, let's get out of his way!" begged Nan.

By this time the elephant was close to the front row of those who had been watching the parade. But those same people who had been in the front ranks, to see all they could, were no longer there. Like the Bobbsey family, they were running away.

Mrs. Bobbsey had hold of Flossie and his father held Freddie's hand. But before they could go very far, so quickly did the elephant come on that, in another moment, he was looming in all his vast bulk right above the small Bobbsey twins and their parents. Bert and Nan had darted to one side, out of the beast's new line of march.

Then, suddenly, a strange thing happened. The elephant reached out with his trunk, thrusting it over Mr. Bobbsey's shoulder and, reaching down with the tip, which was like a big finger, took hold of the bag of warm, brown roasted peanuts in Freddie's hand!

"Oh, stop!" cried Freddie. "Let me alone! Stop!"

"Help! Help!" screamed Mrs. Bobbsey, trying to shield Flossie from what she thought was an attack by the beast.

"Oh, he's taking Freddie's peanuts!" yelled Flossie, laughing now.

That's just what the elephant did! In another instant it had snatched the bag away from the startled Freddie, not in the least harming the little boy, his father, or, for that matter, any of the Bobbseys. Nor did the elephant touch anyone else in the fleeing crowd.

Holding Freddie's bag of peanuts aloft in his trunk, and making a trumpeting noise, which sounded like a great laugh, the elephant swung about and started back for his companions, which had been held in line by their keepers. The circus parade had stopped when this big elephant had run out of the march.

"Oh, he took my peanuts!" wailed Freddie who was very fond of the brown nuts.

"The elephant took Freddie's peanuts!" half sobbed Flossie.

Having got what he went after, the elephant was content now to get back in line. If he had not done so, there were several keepers who would have driven him back with their big sharp hooks.

"What's the idea, Hamba?" cried a keeper as he tapped the creature on one of his big legs. "What do you mean by trying to spoil the circus parade?"

"Get back in line!" ordered another keeper. Hamba was already doing this as quickly as he could, still holding the bag aloft in his trunk.

"He took my peanuts!" cried Freddie, who with his father and the other Bobbseys had now turned back to regain the places at the curb.

"He did?" exclaimed the keeper. "Your peanuts?"

"Yes, he took the whole bag!"

For the first time the circus men became aware of what had really happened. They looked at what Hamba carried in the tip of his trunk.

"That's right!" murmured one of the men. "He's taken the little boy's peanuts!"

"They were hot and freshly roasted," sighed Freddie.

"That accounts for it," chuckled another keeper. "Hamba is crazy about fresh-roasted peanuts. I remember once when I was leading him past a peanut wagon, that he broke away, upset the cart and ate every peanut he could get hold of. He must have smelled this little boy's peanuts and that's why he got out of line."

"Well, he gave us a terrible scare," said Mrs. Bobbsey.

"I'm sorry, lady," spoke the keeper. Then,

as he urged Hamba back among the herd of swaying elephants he added, "I'll tell you what I'll do, little boy. You're coming to the circus, aren't you?"

"Sure!" nodded Freddie.

"Well, then, ask for me in the animal tent. My name is Bill Button and I'm Hamba's keeper. I'll make him do a trick for you."

"Will you, really?" asked Freddie, all excited now.

"I surely will. I can't give you back your peanuts for Hamba has chewed them up." This was true, for the elephant had by this time stuffed peanuts, bag and all, into his mouth and was chewing them and almost smiling, it seemed, because they tasted so good. "No, I can't give you back your peanuts," went on Bill Button, "but I'll make Hamba do a special little trick for you because he was so bad."

"Oh, I guess he wasn't really bad," murmured Flossie, as she with her brothers and sister moved back toward their places in the line. "I guess he was just hungry."

"Hamba is always hungry!" chuckled another keeper.

"Well, he certainly made a grand rush for Freddie's peanuts," remarked Mrs. Bobbsey. "Now, children, get back in your places, if you can find them, and we'll watch the rest of the circus parade."

"Oh, there's somebody on our stepping-stone!" cried Flossie as they made their way to where they had been standing before. It was true. Two big boys had taken the places where Flossie and Freddie had had such a good view of the free show up to the time the elephant had run away.

"Make 'em get off our stone, Daddy!" begged Freddie.

"Well, I don't know that I can do that," said Mr. Bobbsey. "You see, we gave up our places to get away from the charging elephant. So whoever came along next had a right to them."

However, things turned out nicely for the Bobbsey twins. A big policeman, who knew the children, heard the talk of Flossie and Freddie and, going up to the big boys on the stone, the officer said:

"Here! You chaps are tall enough to see over the heads of the crowd. But these little people aren't. Let them get back on their stone."

"Sure!" said one big boy, smiling.

"We were only holding the place for them," said the other.

They got down and moved away. Then, when Freddie and Flossie climbed back up onto the stone, Nan and Bert managed to squeeze in behind them, and Mr. and Mrs. Bobbsey also found places where they could view the remainder of the parade.

There was still much of the parade to be seen, and the children were delighted with the sights. It was not, by any means, the first circus parade they had watched, but the latest one was always the best, it seemed.

At last, after many more wheeled cages of animals had rumbled along the street, and another herd of camels had swayed past, and another gay van of clowns had made the crowd laugh, there came the end of the procession, the tooting Calliope, or "steam piano."

"I wish I could play that!" murmured Flossie as she and the others saw one man shovel coal into the boiler to make steam while the other touched the keys that made the music.

"You have to be a fireman to play that!" declared Freddie. "I'm going to be a fireman when I grow up and I'm going to play a steam piano just like that."

"Oh, dear!" sighed Nan as the music maker turned down the next street out of sight, but not out of sound. "Oh, dear!"

"What's the matter?" asked Bert as the Bobbsey family prepared to go back home.

"It's all over," Nan said. "I was thinking so much about how lovely the parade would be—and it was wonderful—but now it's all over and we won't see another for more than a year."

"No," agreed Bert with a laugh, "we won't. But we'll go to the real circus this afternoon. We'll see the animals and some of the side-shows and we'll be in the main tent and watch the bareback riders and the trapeze artists and everything like that. It'll be great!"

"Yes," said Nan, "I guess it will. I'm silly to care just because the parade is gone."

After a hurried and early luncheon at home, Mr. and Mrs. Bobbsey prepared to take the twins to the circus grounds. They all wanted to leave early so they could have plenty of time to see everything.

"We can go to the side-show first," suggested Bert as they were on their way. "That's always open, but the main performance doesn't start until after two o'clock."

"Yes, I suppose you'll want to take in that part," chuckled Mr. Bobbsey. "I always did when I was a boy."

There was a big crowd at the circus grounds when the Bobbsey twins arrived, early as it was. The hopes of Bert and his chums of earning free tickets by watering the elephants had not been realized. A few boys had carried water, before the circus men ran a hose line from a city hydrant and so had all the water they needed. But instead of being given tickets, the boys were handed dimes, and not enough of them came to any one lad to permit him to buy a ticket.

The trouble the circus had had before coming to Lakeport had been straightened out now and all the tents were up and everything was in the usual order. Though the children had been to the grounds many times while the circus was being put in order, still this visit, when they were to see the real performance, thrilled them very much.

They looked at the gay banners in front of the side-show tent. There was the fat lady, the living skeleton, the strong man who was pictured lifting a horse, and a lady with many snakes twined around her arms and legs. The end picture showed a man making a number of dogs do tricks.

"That's what I want to see!" exclaimed Freddie. "The dog show."

"Yes, we'll look at that," Bert agreed. "Maybe we can see some new tricks to teach Waggo and Snap."

"I want to see the human mermaid," murmured Nan, for there was a sign and picture about the "human fish," as she was called. "I want to see how long she can stay under water." Nan was much interested in swimming since she had spent some time at a girls' camp where swimming was featured.

"I want to see the fat lady," said Flossie. "Maybe when I grow up," she added, "I'll be a fat lady in a circus."

"Oh, I hope not!" exclaimed Mrs. Bobbsey, laughing.

Into the side-show tent hurried the Bobbsey twins, eager to see all that was being offered. A crowd followed, for since it was too early for the main performance to start, the best thing that could be done was to view the side-shows.

"This way! This way!" called the manager, as he took his place on the platform. There sat a man, gay in a glittering, spangled suit, while about him lay a number of trick dogs.

"This way, folks!" shouted the manager again. "You are about to observe Professor Mungo exhibit his marvelous and wonderful collection of trained canines."

"*Canines!*" murmured Freddie. "They look just like *dogs*."

"*Canine* is the Latin word for dog," explained Mrs. Bobbsey.

"Oh," said Freddie. "I'm glad of that."

"This way! This way, folks!" cried the manager. "All ready, Professor Mungo," he went on as the crowd gathered about the dog platform. "Let's go!"

The spangled man got up. But instead of calling on his dogs to do some tricks, Professor Mungo walked to the edge of the platform and, looking down at Freddie Bobbsey, said to the manager:

"There's the boy now! There's the boy who has the dog we want!"

There was a strange feeling in the heart of Freddie, and also in that of Flossie. Even Nan and Bert looked a little frightened.

CHAPTER X

AMONG THE ANIMALS

"What's this? What's this?" asked the side-show manager who had been telling about the different acts in the tent. "You say this boy has one of your trick dogs, Professor Mungo?"

"No, I didn't exactly say that," answered the spangled man as he leaned over the edge of his platform and kept looking at Freddie. "But he has a trick dog we must get."

"You can't have my dog!" cried the little Bobbsey boy. "No, Sir!"

"Don't let him take Waggo!" cried Flossie.

Some of the trick dogs on the platform, hearing loud voices, began to yap and bark. A few, thinking it was time for them to start performing, began to do their tricks. One dog began to climb a ladder while another rang a bell that swung on a pole, taking hold of a rope that was fastened to the bell clapper.

"I must have that trick dog!" exclaimed

Professor Mungo. This name was not his real name, only his circus title.

"No! No!" wailed Flossie.

"He shan't have our Waggo!" declared Freddie.

"Of course he shan't!" echoed Nan, trying to comfort Flossie who was almost crying. Bert kept close to Freddie and said to the dog man:

"What do you mean by this talk? We have a trick dog, but he isn't yours."

"I know he isn't mine," said Professor Mungo, and he smiled a little. "But I want him to be mine and this little fellow, the other day, said he might sell me the dog. I had a good trick dog die on me and I need a new one. I'll buy yours if he's any good."

"Oh, Waggo is good—he's very good!"

"But we aren't going to sell him!" declared Freddie.

"You said you would!" answered the man in tights and spangles.

"I know I did, but I'm not going to now," Freddie repeated.

"We're going to keep our dog and have a circus of our own," stated Bert.

By this time Mr. and Mrs. Bobbsey had come close to the children. The parents had moved a little away from the twins to watch the snake charmer take her serpents from their blanket to be ready for her part in the show. Now, hearing the talk between Professor Mungo and Freddie, Mr. Bobbsey asked:

"What's all this about?"

He was soon told but he was not worried, though Freddie and Flossie had been just a little afraid as they might lose Waggo.

"Of course, if the boy doesn't want to sell his dog, that ends it," said the manager.

"I'd like to buy a good trick dog to take the place of the one that died," added the trainer. "Any time you want to sell your Waggo, as you call him, I'll give you a good price. Think it over. Our show will be here for a couple of days yet."

"We'll never sell Waggo!" declared Freddie.

"Never!" echoed Flossie.

"We have a regular menagerie," added Nan. "Our old dog and cat came back and we're going to teach them tricks."

"We'll have a little circus of our own," concluded Bert.

"Well, don't start opposition to us!" chuckled the manager. "We have had trouble enough. Wait until we pull out before you start your show."

"I guess we'll have to," said Bert with a smile. "It will take a while to teach Snap and Snoop some tricks, but Waggo knows a lot already."

"Well, now I'm going to put my dogs through their tricks," said Professor Mungo to the children. "You may watch and maybe you'll learn how to teach your pets some new ones. All ready, now! Here we go!" he cried in a loud voice. The crowd, including the Bobbsey twins, drew nearer to the platform, the trainer blew a whistle and his dogs gathered about him, taking their positions on little stools, platforms, or small chairs placed about the stage.

Then Professor Mungo, as he was called, put his animals through their tricks. First they did ordinary stunts, such as walking on their front and hind legs, turning somersaults, jumping through paper-covered hoops, climbing ladders, and ringing several bells.

"And now," suddenly announced the trainer, "I will show you my Red Cross dogs in a wonderful act."

He took some of the animals behind a little curtain and in a few minutes they trotted out again. Two of the dogs, made to look like little horses, were hitched to a small wagon that was a copy of a real ambulance. On the seat was a driver dog and on the back step a dog dressed in a white suit like a hospital doctor.

Another dog, which was not attired in any way, trotted to the middle of the stage and stretched out as if hurt. Then the two dogs hitched to the ambulance drew it toward the "injured" animal, the bell clanging just as it does on a real hospital ambulance. Reaching the make-believe injured dog, the ambulance stopped, the "doctor" and the "driver" got down, took hold of the other dog in their teeth, one at the front feet and the other at the hind feet. On the sick dog's paws were leather straps so he could be lifted easily by his canine friends.

Then, to the delight of the Bobbsey twins

and others in the side-show audience, the "doctor" and his helper dog carried the sick one to the ambulance and drove off with him to the "hospital," the bell clanging loudly.

"That's a fine trick!" said Bert.

"We'll train our dogs and cats to do that!" said Freddie.

"I guess you'll find it hard work," his mother remarked.

"Yes," agreed Mr. Bobbsey. "I think it took Professor Mungo a long time to get his dogs to do this stunt as well as they do."

There were a few more tricks, which the Bobbsey twins decided to use in their own circus. Then the dog show came to a close and the crowd moved around the tent to the next platform where sat a very fat and jolly lady, selling her photographs. The fat lady did no tricks.

"She's just there to be looked at," Nan said.

Next to her was a very thin and bony man called the "living skeleton," and he did nothing but sell his pictures.

The snake "charmer," however, was very active, as she let the living serpents twine about her, and this seemed to please the crowd. So did the act of the strong man who put iron chains around his arms and broke them with his swelling muscles.

"I'd like to be as strong as he is," murmured Bert.

"So would I," echoed Freddie. "Then, if my fire engine got stuck in a snowdrift when I was driving it to a real fire, I could lift it out and save the building. For I'm going to be a real fireman when I grow up," he said.

The Bobbsey twins greatly enjoyed all the sights in the side-show and when at last they came out, it was one o'clock. The main performance in the "big top" would start about two o'clock.

"Then we'll have time to see the animals in the menagerie tent before the show begins," said Mrs. Bobbsey.

"Oh, what a wonderful day we're having!" murmured Nan.

"Dandy!" echoed Bert.

"Let's go see the elephants!" cried Freddie. "I've two bags of peanuts for 'em."

"So have I!" exclaimed Flossie, for the small twins had insisted upon buying this treat for the big animals before going in.

"We'll find that Mr. Bill Button. He said he'd let me feed Hamba because he took my other bag of peanuts when I didn't want him to," went on Freddie.

"We'll come to the elephants in time," Mrs. Bobbsey said. "There are other animals to see. Take your time and look at all of them."

Though the children were interested in the cages of tigers, lions, bears and other wild beasts, and though they marveled at the tall giraffes, they were eager to get to the elephant section. So toward the big, swaying beasts they soon made their way.

"There he is! There's Hamba!" cried Flossie, pointing to the elephant that had run away in the parade.

"And I see Mr. Bill Button!" cried Freddie. "Here we are!" he called to the keeper.

"So I see!" chuckled the elephant man. "Well, Hamba is glad to see you. He's behaving himself now. Hi, Hamba! Salute!" cried Bill Button. At once the elephant raised his trunk in the air and gave a loud, trumpeting cry.

"Oh," murmured Flossie, "is he going to run away again?"

"No," chuckled Bill Button. "That's just his way of saying 'Hello!' to you children. That's the trick I promised you. And it also means he likes peanuts!" added the keeper, winking an eye at Mr. and Mrs. Bobbsey.

"We've brought him some!" exclaimed Freddie. He held out one of his bags. Big Hamba at once took it, and with his trunk stuffed the treat into his mouth. The elephant's little eyes seemed to laugh as he munched the roasted nuts.

"Now it's my turn to feed him!" cried Flossie. She held out one of her bags, and Hamba took it quickly.

"He's very hungry," Freddie chuckled. "I'll give him my other bag."

Hamba made short work of this but when Flossie tried to reach out her second bag to the big beast he could not get it in his trunk. The crowd that had gathered about the Bobbsey twins had pushed Flossie farther down the rope barrier so she was not so near Hamba.

"Here, let me have your peanuts. I can hand them to him!" called Freddie. He did not take his eyes off the elephant's swaying trunk, but reached back, groping for Flossie's peanuts.

Freddie grasped something in his hand, pulled it away, and thinking it was the bag of peanuts he had taken from his sister, held it out to Hamba. The elephant took it, but a moment later a woman's voice loudly cried:

"Oh, the elephant has my hand-bag! He has my purse with all my money in it and my ticket home on the railroad and everything. Oh, the elephant has my hand-bag! Make him give it back!"

It was true enough. Clutched in the beast's raised trunk was the woman's purse. Freddie, without looking, had reached back to get Flossie's second bag of nuts. But as Flossie was no longer beside him, Freddie had, without meaning to, taken the woman's hand-bag and fed it to Hamba!

"Oh, don't let him eat it! Don't let him swallow my money!" the woman begged.

Hamba was lowering the purse toward his open mouth.

CHAPTER XI

IN THE BIG TOP

FREDDIE BOBBSEY was as much surprised at what had happened as was the woman, Bill Button, and others in the crowd about the elephants. Even Hamba did not seem to understand what had happened. The big creature had been busy taking bags of peanuts from Freddie and Flossie. When the little boy held out the hand-bag the elephant at first thought it was more peanuts. Freddie thought so himself, not looking at what he was doing.

But an elephant's trunk is his nose and through it he smells things. So it took him only a moment to smell that what he had in his trunk was not peanuts, good to eat, but something strange and not at all appetizing. However, he had started to lower the bag toward his mouth before he realized his mistake.

"Don't let him eat my bag!" cried the

woman again. "It has money in it and tickets and——"

"Don't be worried, lady," said Bill Button with a laugh. "Hamba is smart enough not to eat a pocketbook for peanuts. But I won't take any chances on him tossing it away, or maybe stepping on it, which he might do, thinking the small boy tried to fool him, though I know the little fellow wouldn't do that. Here, Hamba! None of that! Give it here!" the keeper ordered.

He held out his hand, from where he stood within the rope barrier in front of the great beast. Hamba slowly lowered his trunk and put the woman's bag into the hand of Bill Button.

"There you are, lady!" the keeper said, giving her back her property.

"Oh, thank you!" she murmured. "I was so surprised," she went on to those about her, "when I felt this little boy's hand reaching for my purse and the next thing I knew the elephant had it!"

"I—I didn't mean to do it!" stammered Freddie.

"I know you didn't, my dear."

"I was reaching for Flossie's peanuts 'cause she couldn't feed 'em to Hamba herself," Freddie went on. "I took your purse by mistake."

"Here are my peanuts now!" called Flossie, trying to hand the bag through the crowd to her small brother. "Give 'em to the elephant."

"I'll pass 'em for you," offered a jolly man who stood between Freddie and his twin sister. "Let's see what the elephant does with 'em."

"He'll eat 'em, that's what he'll do!" Freddie answered.

This is just what Hamba did, when Freddie gave him the fourth bag of peanuts.

"He's getting more than his share," said Mrs. Bobbsey.

"I'll get some for this little elephant," offered Nan, pointing to the smallest animal in the herd.

He was chained farther back from the ropes than were the others and could not reach out so far with his small trunk. Near the elephant section of the animal tent was a peanut stand. Nan darted there, bought two bags and tossed them to the little elephant who seemed very happy at getting them. Hamba, who was rather greedy, tried to reach over and take them away from his companion. But the heavy chains around Hamba's legs prevented him from doing this.

Others in the crowd were feeding peanuts to the rest of the elephants and the Bobbsey twins looked on in delight until their father reminded them that there were other animals yet to be seen, and that it was getting late.

"The performance will soon start in the big top," Mr. Bobbsey warned the children.

"Then let's go in before somebody takes our seats!" cried Freddie. "I've seen enough elephants."

"Oh, I love to look at them," murmured Nan. "They are so big and noble."

"Let's go see the camels," proposed Bert. "They're funny, I think. They always look as if they were mad or had the toothache or something."

"Do camels eat peanuts?" asked Freddie.

"I don't know," his mother said. "But even if they do you aren't going to buy any more. You've spent enough feeding the animals. They have their own circus food."

The children made the circuit of the animal tent, pausing for a time in front of the snarling, cud-chewing camels, and then went on into the main tent.

"I hope no one has our seats," said Freddie again.

"Our seats are reserved," spoke Nan, who had seen her father buy the tickets. "Nobody can take them except us."

The crowd was now pouring into the main tent and all about could be heard the calls of the ushers and the slamming and banging as they turned down the seats in the reserved section. There was a great clattering noise as those who had places along the planks which formed the cheaper priced seats, climbed up to where they were to sit. After a while all the seats were filled and the Bobbsey twins who, like many other children, had been waiting patiently for the show to start, suddenly heard a burst of music.

"Here comes the grand entry!" cried Bert, who was reading from a program. "It's a pageant of all the nations of the world," he announced.

"What's that mean?" asked Freddie.

"Never mind now," advised his mother. "Look, here comes the procession!"

To the stirring music of the band, stationed near the entrance, there now began circling the arena the horses, camels, elephants and some other animals from the menagerie. All these beasts wore blankets gay in color and glittering with spangles. Men and women, as gaily attired as were the animals, rode on their backs. Around the tent went this colorful parade and then the circus really started.

The Bobbsey twins could not remember half they saw, nor is there room in this book to tell you. There were two rings and three platforms on which, at the same time, many acts took place. Trapeze performers swung through the air, horses pranced as their riders leaped to and fro from their backs. Several big elephants did all sorts of tricks, from almost standing on one another's backs to making a pyramid about their trainer.

"Oh, look at the funny clowns!" cried Freddie in delight as a crowd of these jolly entertainers began leaping about the arena, in and out of the rings and upon the platforms. Some of the clowns were seemingly almost as tall as giants. Others were like fat dwarfs. Their faces were brilliant with red, yellow and blue paint and they wore gaily-colored suits.

Suddenly one tall clown began to chase another clown trying to hit him with a big club. The clown who was running away was short and stout. Seeing that he could not escape, the little clown leaped over the ropes which formed a barrier to the first row of seats, nearest the arena, and began climbing among the spectators.

"I'll get you! I'll get you!" yelled the tall clown in a shrill voice as he followed.

Then, all at once, the little clown leaped to a place on the footboards right in front of Bert and Nan. There, before the eyes of the startled children, the small clown began to puff and swell up like a balloon.

"Oh, look! Look!" cried Nan, "He'll blow up and scatter all over us. Bert, make him go away!"

Bigger and bigger the short clown puffed out and now the tall clown was close to him, having followed him up among the spectators.

"Say! This is great!" shouted Bert, laughing at Nan's dismay. "They're performing specially for us!"

The tall clown raised his big club over the head of the short one who was now as round as a balloon.

"I've got you now!" yelled the tall clown. He banged his club on the fat clown's head.

Suddenly there was a loud explosion.

CHAPTER XII

FLOSSIE IS GONE

BERT and Nan Bobbsey, who had been to
several more circuses than had their small
brother and sister, were so surprised that they
gave loud shouts. As for Flossie she just
screamed, for the fat clown seemed to have
blown apart right in front of her. And Freddie, well, he was so excited that he jumped up
and down in his seat and cried:

"Where is he? Where did he go? Where's
the fat clown?"

There was great excitement in that section
of the tent where the Bobbsey family sat. The
rush of the small clown out of the arena and
up among the seats, the pursuit of the tall
clown, the explosion and the seeming disap-
pearance of the fat fun-maker had taken
everybody by surprise.

"Where is he? Where is he?" cried Freddie
again.

With a laugh that seemed to combine the

cackling of a hen and the crowing of a rooster the tall clown, shaking his club, cried:

"I got him! I got him!"

It really seemed as if he had, for though Flossie and Freddie looked all about, as did Nan and Bert, the fat clown could not be located.

Then suddenly, from beneath the Bobbsey twins, a voice called:

"Here I am! Here I am! Ho! Ho! Ho!"

Looking down through the spaces between the boards that formed the slanting platform on which their seats rested, the twins saw the fat clown hanging by his hands from a pole. But he was no longer fat. His gay suit hung about him in many folds, much too big for him.

"Here I am!" he called again.

Then he pulled himself up by his hands like an acrobat, and wiggling through a space in the boards, stood close to the Bobbsey twins. The children had a near view of the clown and they could see the coarse streaks of paint on his cheeks and nose. He was making funny faces which caused Flossie and Freddie to laugh.

Then Bert and Nan joined in the mirth as did their father and mother and also the people near them. It was all a big joke, or circus trick, as the children now understood. At first Flossie and Freddie had thought the tall clown was really angry at the fat one.

"What made him explode?" asked Flossie, as with another cackling laugh the tall clown ran down an aisle to the arena. He was followed by the fat clown who now had to hold his big suit up about him to prevent it from falling to the floor.

"He was blown up with air," said Bert. "I know how it's done. Under his suit the fat clown had something like a big, toy rubber balloon. That's what made him look so fat. When the tall clown banged him on the head with the club, the balloon burst just as you break a paper bag when it's blown up."

"Was that the way, Daddy?" asked Nan, who was not quite sure.

"Yes," answered her father. "It was all a trick."

"Well, it was fun, anyhow," stated Flossie.

"Lots of fun!" agreed Freddie. "I guess when I grow up," he went on, "I'll be a circus clown instead of a fireman. It's more jolly."

The excitement caused by the rush of the fat clown up among the spectators had now quieted and the Bobbsey twins could give more attention to the other acts of the circus. A troupe of trained horses in charge of a man and a woman dressed all in white now began to perform in the ring directly in front of the children. Between glimpses of these animals the children saw, across the arena, the fat clown once more blowing himself up with air through a long rubber tube he held in his mouth. Then the tall clown chased him up among the seats again and once more there was the "explosion," followed by shouts of laughter. It was a good trick and the two funny clowns were much applauded.

The trained horses gave an act in which Mr. and Mrs. Bobbsey were much interested, but Freddie and Flossie said they would much rather see the elephants.

"Or even the dogs," added Flossie. "Only dogs don't eat peanuts."

"And they don't take hand-bags, either," chuckled Bert.

There were so many jolly and exciting

things to see at the circus that it is no wonder the children could not remember half of them to talk about afterward. As it was the younger twins would be looking at horses, while Bert and Nan would, perhaps, be watching a band of Japanese acrobats. One of these men tossed a boy up and down in the air, catching him on his feet and throwing him across the platform to another man who caught him on his feet. He, like the other man, lay on his back, legs in the air. The boy twirled like a ball. Then these Japanese performers tossed barrels in the same manner.

"Look! Look!" cried Nan, all excited. "Look, Flossie and Freddie! Aren't those Japanese wonderful?"

The small twins were just then looking at a model of a house which was being set up in a ring in front of them. When the house was completed and several persons were inside, suddenly clouds of smoke rolled out and there were flashes of flame.

"Why, it's a fire!" cried Freddie. "Oh, it's a real fire!"

It was not, of course; just another trick,

but from the manner in which the persons in the model house acted, running about and yelling, it seemed like a real fire.

Then came a clanging of bells and the tooting of a shrill whistle and Freddie, looking down the arena, cried:

"Oh, here comes the engine! Oh, I'm going to be a fireman! I'm going to help put out the fire!"

"No you aren't!" exclaimed his father, grasping the little boy just in time to prevent him from scurrying down the slanting aisle. "This is only part of the circus act. Sit still and watch it."

Much against his will, Freddie settled back in his seat and watched. There was a small, but real fire engine, of an old-fashioned type, drawn by real horses, and as it reached the scene of the fire some clowns, dressed as firemen, unreeled the hose and the water began to spurt.

"Oh, it's real water! It's real!" shouted Freddie in delight. "It squirts real water just like my toy fire engine," which, as a matter of fact, it did.

The clown firemen, however, seemed more

eager to douse one another with the stream from the hose than to play the water on the "burning" house. Meanwhile the people in the little house grew wildly excited. More smoke rolled out, the red flames grew brighter and finally several other clowns leaped from the roof of the house.

They did not get hurt, for they landed on big cushions, like the springs of a bed, and bounced up in the air several times, all the while shouting and whooping. First one clown would have the hose, spraying water on the clown next to him. Then another clown would grab the nozzle and send the water in the face of a man who was trying to climb out of a window of the "burning" house.

Then ladders were raised to the side walls, which some clown firemen scaled. But as they got to the middle the ladders broke and the clowns fell on the spring cushions bouncing up and down. One clown did manage to reach the roof and, grabbing what seemed to be a woman, started down the ladder with her to save her from the flames. Another clown on a different ladder made a grab for the woman and the two pulled so hard that she came apart.

"Oh!" screamed Nan.

"It's only a dummy!" chuckled Bert, and so it was, a dressed figure stuffed with sawdust.

All of a sudden the four walls of the house and the roof fell in and from the ruins leaped the clown firemen and the clown inmates of the house, dancing around the structure and singing. The water ceased spraying, the smoke rolled away, the flames died out and with clanging bells the engine was hauled off the scene.

The destruction of the house had been only make-believe, of course, the smoke and flames coming from Fourth of July red fire burned inside. But it created lots of fun and Freddie, with wide open eyes, murmured:

"I wish they'd do it all over again."

"You don't want much for one admission ticket!" chuckled his Father.

The circus performance was now drawing to a close, as could be told when men began circulating among the spectators, calling:

"Get your tickets for the grand concert.

Only twenty-five cents! Concert starts immediately after the last race! Here you are!"

"Oh, may we stay to the concert?" asked Nan.

"I want to hear it!" begged Freddie.

"Well, we might as well see it all," agreed Mr. Bobbsey.

"Here you are! Get your tickets!" shouted the usher. "Holders of reserved seats may remain where they are. The grand concert takes place immediately after the last race now about to start. Twenty-five cents. Hear the grand band and the sweet singers. See the wonderful sights of the grand concert! Get your tickets now. Only a few left."

Mr. Bobbsey bought some tickets and then the children, more than ever delighted with the day's outing, settled down to watch the races. These were exciting enough. Several men on horses rushed shouting about the arena, the ribbon streamers they wore on their heads fluttering in the wind caused by the speed of their horses. A man on a black horse won. Then some women raced and the rider of a white horse received the flag trophy.

There was a dog race and an elephant race, and this latter the Bobbsey twins thought the most exciting of all as the big beasts really lumbered pretty fast about the arena circle, the men sitting upon the heads of the immense creatures and urging them on with loud shouts.

Last of all came the chariot races, four horses being hitched abreast to the ancient, rumbling, two-wheeled vehicles. They went so fast around the turns that the chariots skidded in the dirt and one nearly overturned while the spectators held their breaths and Nan found herself clutching the arm of the man next to her, thinking, in her tense excitement, that she had hold of Bert.

"There's no danger," the man said with a laugh as Nan realized her mistake.

So it proved, for the chariots rumbled and thundered safely about the arena and a fine appearing man in a bright blue suit, dressed as were the ancient Romans, won the race.

"Whew! That was exciting!" murmured Bert.

"Wasn't it!" agreed Nan, her cheeks red and her eyes shining.

There was a movement at the circus entrance through which the performers appeared and as the chariots and their panting steeds rolled out of sight a troupe of the concert singers came on. The "Grand Concert" took place on a platform directly in front of the reserved seats where the Bobbsey family had places.

As a concert it did not amount to much, for there were only a few songs by some men and women, accompanied by part of the circus band. The children enjoyed it, however, even if the adults did not. Then, to the delight of Bert, Nan, Flossie and Freddie, the freaks from the side-shows came marching in to be looked at by the crowds.

"Oh, we've seen these," said Mrs. Bobbsey. "I don't think much of this concert. It's a cheat!"

"But we want to see 'em again!" begged Freddie. "Here's the man with the trained dogs."

Sure enough, Professor Mungo and his "canines" gave a short exhibition which the Bobbsey twins watched closely as they were determined to have a circus of their own, in which Snap and Waggo would do at least a few of the tricks shown by the circus man.

"I want to see the fat lady again," Flossie said as this member of the troupe exhibited her plumpness. "I think she's nice!"

"She certainly looks well fed!" chuckled Mr. Bobbsey.

The concert proved to be shorter than the children had hoped it would be, for the "grand fi-nal-lie," as the manager called it, came soon after the dog tricks. Then, as the musicians got up to leave, Mr. Bobbsey said:

"Come on, my dears, it's all over."

"Is that all?" asked Freddie in disappointed tones.

"Yes, but we'll go out through the animal tent and you may look at them again," promised his mother.

This helped some, and the children would have lingered there among the beasts for a long time, if their parents had not gradually urged them on and out by the remark that it was nearly supper time.

There were not many persons in the animal tent now, as only part of the crowd had remained for the concert. It was easier to get a good view of the elephants, camels, lions, tigers and other jungle creatures.

"I wish we had some more peanuts for Hamba," murmured Freddie as he paused in front of the big elephant.

"You've fed him plenty," said his father. "Come on now, all of you. There's been enough circus for one day!"

They moved outside the animal tent and were near the side-shows when Mrs. Bobbsey suddenly exclaimed:

"Where's Flossie?"

"Isn't she with you?" asked Nan.

"No. I saw her with you a moment ago, just as we were coming out. But now—Oh, dear! Flossie is lost!"

CHAPTER XIII

LUCKILY the Bobbseys had come from the circus tent after the largest part of the crowd had left, so they were not in the press and confusion that might have been milling about them when most of the audience had rushed out. Consequently, there was room for them to move about easily in the clear spaces. Mrs. Bobbsey now rapidly looked at one after another of these open spaces, hoping she might find her little girl. But Flossie was not to be seen.

"Oh, dear!" sighed Mrs. Bobbsey.

"What's the matter?" asked Mr. Bobbsey, who with Bert was watching a couple of men adjust some tent pegs that had loosened.

"Flossie is lost!" answered his wife.

"No!" he exclaimed, hardly believing. "Why, she was with us a moment ago."

"I know it," agreed his wife. "But she either wandered away or was caught in a crowd and rushed off. Oh, where can she be?"

"We'll find her!" said Mr. Bobbsey.

"We'll all look," added Nan.

"There isn't such a crowd now," went on Mr. Bobbsey. "It will be easy to find her. I'll ask some of the police."

There were a number of Lakeport officers about the circus grounds to keep order, but now, as the performance was over, they had little to do. Seeing one of these policemen whom he knew, Mr. Bobbsey went up to him and said:

"My little girl is lost."

"Oh, is that so, Mr. Bobbsey?" asked the policeman who had often been on duty near the lumber-yard. "Which one? Nan or Flossie?"

"It's Flossie," exclaimed Mrs. Bobbsey while Nan murmured:

"I guess I'm big enough not to get lost."

"Oh, Flossie!" went on the officer. "Yes, I know that fat little blue-eyed child. Now don't worry! She can't be much lost and we'll soon find her. There's been no accident, so you can make your mind easy on that score, Mrs. Bobbsey," he said earnestly.

"I'm glad of that. But where can Flossie be?"

"Maybe," exclaimed Freddie, "she's feeding peanuts to the elephants. They eat a lot."

"Indeed they do!" chuckled the officer. "Well, we'll go back in the animal tent and look."

He led the way toward the main entrance, but Mrs. Bobbsey said:

"I hardly think she can be among the elephants. We just came out and she was with us."

"She may have slipped back amongst 'em, unbeknown to you, Ma'am," said the officer. "We'll have a bit of a look and then we'll know for sure."

"I'll go with Officer Chadman, Mary," said Mr. Bobbsey to his wife. "You and the other children look around outside here until we return."

"Oh, I do hope you find her!"

"We'll go look for her around here," offered Bert, nodding at Nan.

"No!" objected his mother. "You two stay here with me. First thing I know one of you will be lost."

"Not much chance of that!" Bert said, but he did as his mother told him, meanwhile remaining at her side with Nan, the three of them roving their eyes about the crowds that still were moving about near the side-show tent and the "big top." Freddie also helped look for his sister.

Flossie was not to be seen, and when Mr. Bobbsey and the policeman came out to report that the little girl was not feeding the elephants, Mrs. Bobbsey grew more worried.

"Now don't take it so hard, Ma'am," begged the policeman. "I'll ask some of the others if they have seen her. There's a lot of us officers here today and it would be strange if a little girl like Flossie, who is known to most of us, could slip away and be lost. We'll find her for you, have no fear."

Seeing another policeman over near the side-show tent, Mr. Chadman called to him:

"Jim, have you seen anything of a little girl that's lost?"

"I've seen about a dozen lost little girls today," was the answer. "I got 'em all sorted out proper with their right mothers. What sort of a little girl are you looking for?"

"She has blue eyes and light hair," Nan said.

"She's my twin sister and she looks like me!" added Freddie.

"Her name is Flossie Bobbsey!" called Bert.

"See anything of her?" asked the first officer.

"A little girl like that just went in here," said Policeman Jim Tredmore. "I saw her, plain, but I thought she was with a man and woman who went in ahead of her. She's in the side-show, I'm sure!"

The side-shows, unlike the circus, gave a sort of continuous performance, lasting all afternoon and evening. The ticket-seller was still on duty and the "barker" was outside urging the still-remaining crowd to enter and see "the most marvelous aggregation of human freaks and curiosities ever gathered into one tent."

"Here you are—get your tickets!" cried the seller as Mr. and Mrs. Bobbsey hurried toward the entrance.

"It's all right, they're looking for a lost child," explained Policeman Chadman.

"Then pass in, and I hope you find her," murmured the ticket man, not asking any admission price for Mr. Bobbsey and his wife.

"You and Nan stay outside with Freddie," Mrs. Bobbsey called to the other twins. "You might see Flossie wandering around."

The parents of the missing Flossie had no sooner entered the side-show tent than they caught sight of their little daughter. There was not much of a crowd inside and a good view could be had. Flossie was standing in front of the platform on which, in an extra heavy chair, sat the big, rosy fat lady.

"Oh, Flossie!" cried her mother. "What are you doing here?"

"I—I'm learning to be a fat lady in a circus," Flossie answered with dignity.

"Well," chuckled her father, "you've picked out a big job for yourself, my little fat fairy, but you've a good model," and he looked at the freak on the raised platform.

"How did you get in here, Flossie?" asked her mother.

"I—I just walked in," Flossie answered. "After we came out of the circus I thought how Freddie was going to be a fireman and then I thought I could be a fat lady, so I came in to ask her how she got that way."

By this time the freak who had been selling a few of her pictures while waiting for the announcer to get around to her, noticed the Bobbseys.

"What's all this?" she asked with a jolly smile.

"My little girl got separated from us and we thought she was lost," Mrs. Bobbsey said. "We found her here just now admiring you."

"I'm going to be a fat lady in a circus when I grow up!" Flossie declared in her high, piping voice.

"Oh, are you, my dear?" asked the freak, leaning over the edge of the platform to look down and see Flossie. "Well, take my advice and don't. It's a hard life."

"You look as if you enjoyed it," Mr. Bobbsey said, while Mrs. Bobbsey clasped Flossie's hand to make sure she would not wander away again.

"Well, I make the best of it," said Madame Rosalie, which was the fat lady's circus name, "though it isn't easy to get around. As for chairs, I'm afraid to sit in one that isn't specially made for me," she added with a chuckle, and the chair on which she sat creaked as she moved, strong as it was.

"I hope my little girl didn't annoy you," Mrs. Bobbsey said.

"Oh, no indeed. Not at all. I was just noticing that she was staring at me pretty hard when you came along. But then, I'm used to being stared at!" chuckled Madame Rosalie, her fat sides shaking in her mirth.

"Well, I guess you've seen enough, Flossie," her mother said. "You shouldn't have run away from us."

"I didn't run, I just walked," Flossie said.

"It's all the same," her mother answered, trying not to smile. "But come with us now. We are going home."

"I want to see the trained dogs again," Flossie begged.

"No," her father told her, "we must be getting home."

"Here, take this with you with my compliments!" exclaimed the fat lady. Leaning over the edge of the platform, she handed Flossie a large photograph of herself.

"Oh, thank you!" murmured the little girl.

"Very kind of you," said Flossie's mother. Flossie looked at the smiling picture.

"I'm going to be like that when I grow up," she said.

"Oh, I hope not!" whispered Mrs. Bobbsey.

Then, with her father and mother, the little girl hurried outside the side-show tent to find Freddie, Bert and Nan anxiously waiting, for they had been unable to trace the lost one.

"Oh, Flossie! Where have you been?" gasped Nan.

"Learning to be a fat lady," was the answer, and Bert laughed.

"Well, we certainly have had a full day," said Mr. Bobbsey as he reached home with his family that evening. "Dinah has supper all ready."

"Did mah honey lambs hab a good time?" she asked the children.

"Wonderful," said Flossie, holding the fat lady's picture.

"Dandy!" exclaimed Freddie.

"Just too nice for anything," was Nan's opinion.

"And I'm going again tonight!" cried Bert.

"No, indeed, you aren't!" his father quickly said. "One circus a day is enough. Besides, the show won't be there."

"Oh, yes," Bert answered. "It's going to stay two or three days more. But mayn't I go down to the lot with some of the boys after supper, if I don't go in?"

"If you don't stay too late," his father finally agreed.

So, while Flossie, Freddie and Nan went early to bed to dream about the wonderful sights they had seen that day, Bert went again with John and Charlie to the circus lot. They saw the flashing lights and watched the crowds pouring into the tent. Though all three boys had seen the show that afternoon they wanted to go again. But they had no money with which to buy tickets. However, there were a few sights that interested them, while now and then, through openings in the canvas, they had glimpses of what was going on inside.

The next two days while the circus remained in Lakeport were busy ones for the Bobbsey twins. They went many times to the lot where the white tents, gay with colored flags and banners, gleamed in the sun, but they did not go in either the side-show or the main one. However, they were kept busy and amused, while seeing so much of the big circus made them more eager than ever to have a small one of their own.

"We must teach Waggo some more tricks!" decided Bert.

"And we ought to make Snap do a few," added Nan.

"Yes, and maybe the cats, too," Bert said. "Come on, we'll see if Waggo can be trained to walk up a ladder like Professor Mungo's dogs."

With the help of Sam, the colored man of all work, Bert made a small wooden ladder, and after several tries Waggo was able to climb up easily.

"That's a fine, new trick!" cried Freddie.

"And I've taught Snoop to sit up in a corner," said Flossie.

"Have you, really?" asked Nan, surprised to hear this.

"Yes," answered the little girl. "Come and see."

Sure enough, when she propped Snoop up in a corner, the big, old cat sat there on her hind legs for several seconds.

"It's a good trick," Bert decided, " 'cause it's harder to make cats do tricks than it is dogs. We must make Snap do something."

Bert and Nan were busy putting Waggo through his tricks on the side porch, and they were remarking that in another day or so the big circus would travel on, when all of a sudden they heard Freddie shouting. They could not make out what he was saying.

"What's the matter?" asked Bert as Waggo descended the ladder.

"Come and see! Oh, come quick!" cried the little boy.

"I guess he's in trouble again!" murmured Nan.

CHAPTER XIV

THE CIRCUS GOES AWAY

BERT and his sister hastened around the side of the house, for the voice of Freddie had come from that direction. Ahead of them ran Waggo, the trained dog.

"I hope he isn't hurt," said Bert.

"It sounded as if he were in some kind of mischief," sighed Nan.

Again Freddie's voice echoed:

"Come here! Come here, quick!"

Rounding the house corner, Bert and Nan saw their small brother sitting on the grass with Snap beside him. Freddie did not appear to be in any sort of trouble, but Snap was panting, his red tongue lolling from his mouth as if he had been running.

"What's the matter?" asked Bert.

"Why did you yell?" Nan inquired.

"I want you to see what Snap can do," Freddie replied.

"I don't see him doing anything except

panting," observed Bert Bobbsey, annoyed

"You should see what he was doing," Freddie went on. "I've taught him a trick!"

"What kind of a trick?" Nan wanted to know.

"Walking on his hind legs like Waggo," declared the little boy. "I tried to make him walk on his front legs, but I guess he's too big and heavy for that. But he can walk on his hind legs fine! He was doing it when I hollered to you but you didn't get here in time to see him."

"I don't believe he can do that trick," observed Bert. "You just thought he was doing it, Freddie."

"No, he really did it!" insisted the small twin. "Here, I'll show you. Get up, Snap!" he ordered.

Slowly the old, big dog, who had been a pet in the Bobbsey family for a number of years, got to his feet.

"Now watch!" Freddie called.

He took hold of Snap's front paws and partly raised the dog up on his hind legs. Then Snap seemed to know what was wanted of him, for he suddenly settled back, got a good balance and really took a few steps, prancing along on his hind legs.

"Say, that's a dandy trick!" cried Bert.

"Oh, Freddie! You really did it!" exclaimed Nan admiringly.

"No, I didn't do it, Snap's doing it!" Freddie corrected her with a laugh. "But I taught him. First he wouldn't do it, but I patted his head and talked nice to him and told him we'd put him in a play circus and then he did it."

"Well, he certainly did!" exclaimed Bert. "When you think what an old dog he is, it's a grand trick."

"Do you s'pose Freddie really taught Snap that trick?" Nan asked Bert in a low voice as the small boy, once more, made the dog walk along on his hind legs.

"I don't know," Bert replied. "It seems Freddie has a way with him around animals. See how he found out Waggo could do tricks when I never even thought the dog was a trick one."

"But Snap never did any tricks before," objected Nan.

"No," Bert agreed, "but we never tried to

make him. We took it for granted that he couldn't. Maybe he knew how to do this trick before he came to us the first time and maybe, just now, Freddie helped him to remember about it."

"Yes," Nan said. "And perhaps during the time he's been away from us, when we thought he might be dead, Snap was with a circus or in some place where he was taught tricks."

"Maybe," spoke Bert. "If he was taught one trick, maybe he was taught more. We must find out about it. Come here, Snap," he ordered.

The old dog seemed to think he had done enough for a while. And after he had done Freddie's trick, Snap ran away and hid under the porch where it was cool.

"It's hard to teach an old dog new tricks," Bert said, quoting an ancient saying. "But anyhow, Freddie has made a start with Snap. And when he sees Waggo doing some new tricks we're going to teach him, maybe our old dog will wake up and be as clever as the new one."

"Perhaps," said Nan.

Freddie beamed with pride as Bert and Nan told their father and mother, as well as Flossie, at supper that evening, how Snap had walked on his hind legs.

"I think Snap got tired of seeing Waggo do all the tricks, so he decided he'd do a few himself," announced Flossie.

"Maybe," agreed Mr. Bobbsey. "Anyhow, Snap has proved that he can learn something new, even if he is a bit old, and I'm sure you'll have a lot of fun with your pets."

It was harder to teach the cats anything, though Flossie could make Snoop stand in a corner. The "new Christmas cat," as the children called the one about whom part of their Christmas secret had centered, would not do anything.

"She looks pretty when she has a red bow on her neck," Flossie said.

"Well, we'll put her in a cage and pretend she is a tiger," decided Bert. "Anyhow, if we're going to have our circus, it's time we got busy and trained our animals some more. I think I'll ask Dad to let me go to the side-show once again and look at the trick dogs. There are some things I want to find out."

Speaking about this to his father, Bert was given permission to attend the side-show the last night the circus was to remain in Lakeport. So, in company with John and Charlie he hurried to the grounds to view, for the last time, the wonders of the show where the freaks were, but not the performance in the big tent.

To Bert, John and Charlie, though they had seen everything before, it was just as marvelous as it had been the first time. They lingered longest before the platform of the snake "charmer," the place where the strong man was breaking chains on his arm muscles, and where the performing dogs were shown.

"I want to get ideas about some new tricks," Bert explained to his chums. They were as much interested as he was in what Professor Mungo did.

There was an air of unrest and disquiet about the side-shows that neither Bert nor the other boys had noticed before. The performers seemed to hurry through their acts, and as soon as they had finished they slipped off their platforms, going down a little flight of steps at the rear of each one, where they began packing up their trunks and boxes.

"The circus is getting ready to go away," Bert told his chums.

"Let's stay and see 'em take down the tents," proposed Charlie.

"Maybe it'll be too late," Bert objected. "My father told me to be home early."

"I guess he'd let you stay if he knew you were with us," John said. "My folks said I might watch 'em take down the tents. It's great sport. You stay, Bert."

"I'll telephone home and ask if I may," Bert said. They had seen about all there was to be observed in the side-shows, and Bert said he had some new ideas about dog tricks, so they came out. Going to a drug store some distance away from the circus lots, Bert called up his father and received permission to remain with John and Charlie until they had seen the big tent taken down from its poles.

When the boys returned to the grounds they saw that the animal tent was already down, while many of the cages of beasts had been drawn toward the railroad yards where the circus cars were waiting on a side track.

The big tent was still up and it glowed brightly from the gleaming lights within. The strains of the band music floated out into the darkness.

"The circus is going away," remarked Bert a bit sadly.

"Yes," agreed John. "It stayed here longer than usual, and I had a lot of fun at it."

"So did I," said Charlie. "But I sort of hate to see it go."

"I do, too," said Bert. "It's one of the best circuses I've ever seen."

The other boys agreed with this as they wandered about the grounds. The side-show tent was being folded. The performers had already packed up their trappings and gone to the train to get some sleep before they left the town.

Suddenly, as the boys were walking across a dark place in the lots they heard a rumbling sound, a rush of feet and a man's voice yelled:

"Look out, there! Look out for the bulls! Do you want to get trampled on? Out of the way of the bulls!"

CHAPTER XV

WAGGO IS MISSING

"COME on, fellows!" yelled Charlie.

"The wild bulls must be loose!" called John.

He and Charlie started to run, but seeing that Bert Bobbsey did not hasten away, merely turning around to see what all the shouting was about, John called:

"Do you want to get horned by a wild bull, Bert?"

"No, I don't," Bert answered with a laugh. "But I don't believe any wild bulls are coming."

Just then the voice of a circus man shouted again:

"Look out for the bulls!"

"There! Did you hear that?" asked John.

"But look!" added Charlie as he saw black, moving shadows cast by the gasoline flares. "A lot of elephants!"

"The circus men call elephants 'bulls,'" explained Bert. "Bill Button, the keeper of Hamba, told me that the other day."

"Oh, so bulls are only elephants, are they?" asked John.

"That's all," Bert said. "I knew there weren't any wild bulls so I didn't run."

"I'd just as soon get run over by a wild bull as I would by an elephant," said Charlie. "Anyhow, here they come and I guess we'd better get out of their way."

Bert and his chums saw several of the big elephants plunging toward them through the half darkness. The beasts were pushing with their heads some of the heavy circus vans that had settled deep into the soft earth. The eight horses hitched to the wagon had not been able to move it so the "bulls," or elephants, had been called upon.

"See how easy they do it!" exclaimed Bert as the ponderous wagon, with the horses still hitched to it and a man on the seat to guide it, went rumbling past, the elephants at the rear pushing it along the ground.

"I guess it's only like a feather to them," John said.

"Sure," Bert agreed. "I wish," he added as

he and the other two boys stood aside to let the van and elephants pass, "I wish we had some elephants for our circus."

"Are you really going to have one?" asked John.

"Sure!" Bert answered.

"You ought to see his new dog Waggo do tricks," spoke Charlie. "He's great!"

"Yes, he's pretty good," Bert admitted. "We're teaching him more tricks, and Snap, our old dog, is learning some. But he'll never be as smart as Waggo."

"Waggo is worth a lot of money, isn't he?" asked Charlie.

"I guess he is," Bert admitted.

"You'd better be careful of him," advised John.

"Why?" Bert wanted to know as the boys, having watched the elephant push the van out on solid ground, turned to see other sights of the departing circus. "Why should we be careful of Waggo?"

"If he's a valuable trick dog," went on John, "somebody might take him."

"Lots of men and boys, too, would be glad to get a trick dog," added Charlie.

"Well," said Bert, "there's one man right in this circus who would like to get Waggo, but we aren't going to sell him."

"What man?" asked John.

"Professor Mungo, who has the trained dogs," answered the Bobbsey boy. "He asked Freddie to sell Waggo, but my little brother and sister wouldn't, though at first they wanted to."

"Well, keep good watch over that dog," advised Charlie.

"I shall," Bert promised. "But I guess Freddie and Flossie watch him so closely that nothing could happen to him. Oh, look, there's another wagon stuck!" and he pointed to where some men, with two teams of horses, were trying to haul a big van out of a soft place on the circus grounds.

"That's the cage they have the hippopotamus in!" cried John. "I remember it. Say, the hippo is mighty heavy, and he has a tank of water in that van. I guess they won't get it out of the hole with only horses to pull!"

"You're right—they won't!" Bert exclaimed. "Look, here come the bulls again!"

Two big elephants lumbered their way

toward the stalled van which did indeed contain the big hippo in his tank of water. The horses strained as the men urged them to pull, but it was of no use.

"Out of the way!" cried the elephant man. "My bulls will do the trick. Push, Rantan! Come on, Hamba!"

"Why, that elephant is our Hamba!" exclaimed Bert.

"Do you know him?" asked Charlie.

"Well, I guess I know him as much as anybody can know an elephant when one sees him in the circus," chuckled Bert. "My little brother and sister fed him peanuts and Freddie almost fed him a lady's hand-bag by mistake," and he laughed as he told his chums the story.

Now the boys ceased talking as they once more watched the "bulls" push the van out on solid ground. Then the horses were able to pull it and the elephants swayed off to find other work to do about the grounds.

The circus was rapidly breaking up. The side-show tent, the various smaller tents about the grounds and many of the vans were already out of the way. Only the "big top" remained, and as the boys neared it they heard the stirring music which told them that the last of the races was in progress. These were cut short, the "grand concert" was omitted, and almost before the last of the audience had filed out of the big tent men began loosening the ropes. Soon the snowy canvas house began to come down slowly.

"Lively now, men!" called the foreman, and the boys watched as the big poles were loaded upon long vans and the canvas, which was in sections, was folded and laced together by scores of workers.

"That was quick work!" exclaimed Bert, as after what seemed only a few minutes, though it was really longer than that, the big tent was on its way to the next place, where the circus was to show.

"It's getting late," said Charlie. "I guess we'd better go home."

"There isn't anything more to see, anyhow," declared Bert. "The circus is over. No more fun like it for another year."

"Well, it was good while it lasted," chuckled John.

"Sure!" Charlie agreed.

The boys were walking homeward across the end of the grounds on a path that led to the place where the circus train was waiting for the last van to be rolled on the flat cars. Then it would puff on its way. Several circus performers, or men connected with the show, who seemed to have lingered longer than most of their companions, were heading for the train. As the boys stood watching the long strings of cars, some gaily lighted, a voice hailed them.

"Hello!" called a man. "Aren't you the lad who had the trick dog for sale?"

As he stopped to light a match for his cigar the man's face was revealed to Bert, who exclaimed:

"You're Professor Mungo."

"That's right," was the response. "And I guessed right, didn't I, when I said you were the boy who has the trick dog for sale?"

"My brother and my sisters and I own a trick dog named Waggo," Bert answered, "but he isn't for sale. We've changed our minds and we're going to keep him."

"Are you sure?" asked Professor Mungo with a laugh as he blew out a cloud of smoke.

"Am I sure of what?" Bert wanted to know, struck by a sort of hidden meaning in the words.

"Are you sure you don't want to sell that dog?" repeated the circus trainer.

"Oh, yes!" Bert said. "We're going to keep him for our own circus."

"Well, all right!" laughed Professor Mungo, and then he strode off in the darkness.

"I guess he'd like to get Waggo," murmured Charlie.

"He certainly would!" agreed John.

"But he isn't going to!" declared Bert.

He and his chums soon parted, going their various ways. The circus train rumbled on through the night and Bert Bobbsey went to bed.

He was awakened early the next morning by hearing Freddie's shouts down in the yard.

"What's the matter?" called Bert from his window.

"Come down! Come down quick!" begged Freddie. "Waggo is gone!"

CHAPTER XVI

BERT BOBBSEY lost no time putting on his clothes. He did not stop to put all of them on —just his shirt and his trousers, and then in his bare feet he raced down the hall toward the back stairs. This was the shortest way to get to the rear door to reach the yard where Snap and Waggo had their kennels.

"What's the matter, Bert?" asked Nan, looking from her room through the half-open door as she heard her brother's pattering feet. "Is the house on fire? I heard Freddie yelling. I hope that if there is a fire he isn't trying to put it out with his toy engine."

"There isn't any fire!" answered Bert as he ran along. "But Freddie says Waggo is gone!"

"Gone where?" Nan wanted to know.

"Freddie didn't say, but from the way he's yelling I guess he means our dog has run away or has been stolen."

"Stolen!" gasped Nan. "Oh, that's too bad! Who took him? Are you going to chase them? Wait for me!"

Bert did not wait. He was now sliding down the back stair banister railing as the quickest way of reaching the bottom. He did not mean to be impolite to Nan, but this was something that needed to be done in a hurry —the tracing of the lost or stolen Waggo, and Bert did not want to lose any time. So he contented himself with calling to his sister:

"Hurry downstairs!"

"That's what I'll do!" decided Nan. Not waiting to dress herself completely, Bert's sister followed him, only she did not slide down the banister rail. Nan used to do this but she thought she was now getting a little too old for such boyish tricks.

Through the kitchen rushed Nan, shortly after Bert had made his hurried trip past Dinah, who was getting breakfast.

"Well, fo' de lan' sakes!" exclaimed the fat, jolly Negro cook as Nan nearly knocked from her hands some eggs with which Dinah was going to make an omelet. "Fo' de lan' sakes! Whut's goin' on? Fust Freddie he come down so early as I neber see him afo'. Den dat boy Bert he rush through mah kitchen an' now come Nan. Eberybody's in a monstorus hurry dis mawnin'. Whut it all about, anyhow?"

"Waggo is gone!" is all Nan took the time to say as she rushed down the back steps to the yard where she could hear Bert and Freddie talking in excited tones.

"Well, fo' de lan' sakes! Dey's mo' fuss ober a dog dan dere is about bustin' de aigs fo' mah omelet!" grumbled Dinah. "But den I cain't blame dem chilluns," she chuckled. "Dey sho' does lub dem dogs. I s'pects Waggo is only run off t' look fo' a bone! He'll come back," she said, and went on with her preparations for breakfast.

Meanwhile Bert was rapidly firing questions at his brother.

"Where's Waggo? How do you know he's gone? When did you see him last? Is Snap here? Where's Snoop? How did you happen to find out Waggo was gone?"

"Say!" exclaimed Freddie who was a little less excited now, "you talk almost as fast as a fireman. Bert!"

"Well, what about our dog?" demanded Bert.

"He's gone, I tell you! Look!" Freddie pointed at the empty kennel—a small one near the larger box that held Snap. Nothing had happened to Snap. He came lazily out to greet the children as Bert and Freddie were talking.

"Gone?" echoed Nan. "Where?"

"That's what I'd like to know," went on Freddie. "I came down early to see him but when I got here he wasn't in the kennel. I called him and I whistled to him, but he didn't come. Then I yelled for you, Bert."

"Yes, I heard you." Bert was rapidly searching about the yard between the Bobbsey house and the garage, but there was no sign of the missing trick dog.

"Why did you come down so early?" Nan wanted to know. "Did you hear a noise, Freddie? Did you think somebody was taking Waggo?"

"No, but I came down early to teach Waggo a few more tricks if I could. I want him to do a lot of stunts in the circus we're going to have. That man in the circus, Professor Mungo, said that early morning was the best time to teach a dog tricks as he was rested after his night's sleep."

"It doesn't look now as if we could have the circus," said Nan a bit sadly. "Waggo was our best trick dog. I don't believe we'll be able to teach Snap many tricks for he's too old. And if Waggo is gone——"

"He's gone, all right," Bert said, coming back from a hasty search during which he had whistled and called again and again. "Waggo is gone!"

"Maybe he just ran off to the woods," suggested Nan. "Snap used to do that every once in a while when we first got him. We can go look for him, can't we?"

"Sure we can!" declared Bert. "Come on, Nan, we'll go now!"

"I'll come too!" offered Freddie.

"No," objected Nan, who was not as impulsive as either of her brothers. "We aren't dressed—at least I'm not—and we'd better get some breakfast."

"Yes, I guess we had," Bert agreed. "But we'll go right after breakfast. We don't want to lose any time. This is too bad!"

"What's the matter?" asked Flossie who, having heard in her room the talk of her brothers and sister, had come down, only partly dressed, to see what was happening.

"Waggo is gone!" exclaimed Bert, Nan and Freddie all at once.

Then suddenly Flossie said:

"I know where he is!"

"Where?" cried the other three twins, all together.

"He ran away to the circus," declared Flossie, just as if she knew all about it.

"What makes you think that?" asked Bert.

"Because," answered his little sister. Then Flossie sat down on the top step, and as she pulled her short dress down as far over her little fat knees as it would stretch she added, "My legs are cold." It was early in the morning and the sparkling dew was still on the grass.

"How do you know Waggo ran off with the circus?" asked Bert as a sudden new thought came into his own mind. " *'Because'* isn't any reason, you know."

"I know it isn't," Flossie said, still trying to cover her legs. "But I'm sure that's where he has gone. He remembered what you said about him, Freddie."

"What did I say?"

"You said you were going to sell him to the circus and Waggo heard you and maybe he thought we didn't love him any more and wanted to get rid of him. So he ran away to join the circus!"

"Dogs don't know what you say about them," Freddie declared. "I did say we might sell him to the circus, but afterward I said we wouldn't—that we'd keep him for our own circus."

"Maybe he didn't hear you say that last part," insisted Flossie. "He just remembered that you said you wanted to sell him and it made him feel bad and he ran off with the circus. The circus went away in the night, didn't it?"

"Yes," admitted Bert, "it did. And do you know, Nan, I believe little Flossie is more than half right?" he went on. "Not that I believe Waggo knew what Freddie said about selling him, but Waggo may have gone with the circus."

"Would he know enough to follow it?"

Nan asked. "It's a long way from here to the circus lots, and the show didn't go away until late last night. How could Waggo know that?"

"I don't mean he went away by himself," Bert said.

"What then?"

"That man took him!"

"What man?" asked Nan.

"Professor Mungo. Listen, I met him last night when I was over on the lots with John and Charlie watching them take down the tents. I met Professor Mungo then and he said we'd be sorry we hadn't sold Waggo to him."

"He said that?" gasped Nan.

"Sure he did! I thought it was funny at the time!"

"Then he surely came here and took Waggo!" Nan declared, and Flossie and Freddie nodded their heads in agreement. Freddie asked:

"What are we going to do about it?"

"We're going to find Waggo!" cried Bert. "I'll follow that circus and get our dog back! Professor Mungo isn't going to keep him!"

"I'll help you!" offered Freddie. "I'll take my fire engine along and squirt water on that man."

There was so much talk and excitement that Mrs. Bobbsey came out on the back steps to learn what it was all about. When she heard the story she said:

"I don't believe any circus man came here and took Waggo. Your dog has probably wandered away and is lost. You may look for him after breakfast, but you cannot follow the circus. That would be impossible!"

"Well, we'll look for Waggo all around here and in the woods and I'll get the fellows to help," said Bert. "But if we don't find him it's pretty certain he's with the circus and we ought to do something about it."

"You must talk to your father about that," Mrs. Bobbsey said. "But first come in and get dressed, all of you, and then you may hunt for the lost dog."

The search was kept up all of that day, Nan and Flossie doing their part as did Bert and his chums. But when evening came Waggo had not been found. The Bobbsey twins felt very sad

Mr. Bobbsey, having gone away so early in the morning that he did not know of the missing dog, heard the story when he came home from his lumber yard that evening.

"So you couldn't find Waggo?" he asked, as the children told of their fruitless search.

"He isn't around Lakeport!" declared Bert. "He's with the circus, I'm sure."

"Well, then," spoke Mr. Bobbsey, "what I say is, 'All aboard!'"

"All aboard for what?" asked Bert as he and the other children looked at their father, who was smiling in a strange way.

"Are you going to get us a new boat?" Nan wanted to know.

"No," her father said, "I meant all aboard in my auto. We'll take the trail after this circus to see if Waggo is with it."

"Do you mean that, Dad?" cried Bert. "Will you take us to follow the circus so we can get our dog?"

"That's just what I'll do!" Mr. Bobbsey said.

"Hurray!" cried Nan and Bert. But Mrs. Bobbsey said:

"Don't tease them, Richard! You know

you can't let them follow that circus! It's miles and miles away from here now."

"I know it is," admitted Mr. Bobbsey. "But just the same, I'm going to take the children in my auto and follow it. And you may come along if you like."

He smiled, but Mrs. Bobbsey did not, as she exclaimed:

"Richard Bobbsey, what do you mean?"

CHAPTER XVII

FOLLOWING THE CIRCUS

Mr. Bobbsey settled himself more comfortably in his easy chair and looked first at his wife and then at the twins. He was smiling in a way which Bert and Nan, at least, knew meant good times were coming.

"Are you serious, Dick," asked his wife after a pause, "when you say you are going to take these children to follow that circus?"

"Well, we aren't exactly going to *follow* the circus," was the answer, "for that would mean going along the railroad after it. It just happens that I have to make an auto trip to Deepdell, which is the town where the circus is going to show next, and I thought, since some man in the circus may have our dog, that I could get it back."

"Oh, that'll be great!" cried Bert.

"If I see that man I'll go right up and take Waggo away from him!" declared Flossie, her blue eyes flashing.

"I'll squirt water on him from my engine!" threatened Freddie.

"Now, now!" cautioned his father, still smiling. "we must not do anything rash or impolite. It seems, from what you tell me, that Waggo is gone. There can be no doubt of that. Now the dog may have wandered away and become lost. He may have followed the circus. It may very well be that some man from the circus, knowing Waggo was a valuable trick dog, took him."

"Professor Mungo!" murmured Bert. "He said he wanted him."

"Well, I shouldn't say that Professor Mungo took Waggo," went on Mr. Bobbsey. "Perhaps some other man connected with the circus, knowing that Professor Mungo needed a trick dog, just picked Waggo up and sold him. But at any rate, since I have to go to Deepdell on business, I thought, if you children wanted to go, I'd take you."

"Sure we want to go!" cried Nan.

"Do I!" echoed Bert, making a cartwheel across the room.

Mrs. Bobbsey continued to look at her husband.

"Are you serious about this?" she asked.

"Oh, yes, indeed," he replied. "I must go to Deepdell, perhaps to be gone several days. It is time the children had a little outing and we can pack up some clothes and have a fine time along the road. The car is big enough and I'd like to have you come, too."

"I'm afraid I can't go," Mrs. Bobbsey said. "I'd like to, though. It sounds very jolly. But I have several club meetings, and besides, Nan is old enough now to look after Flossie and Freddie. Take the children and I'll stay at home, Dick."

"Oh, Mother! You come!" pleaded Nan.

"Yes, do!" begged Flossie and Freddie, putting their arms around Mrs. Bobbsey.

"Well, I'll see about it," she replied. "Now we must talk about ways and means and plans and all that. When do you expect to start, Dick?"

"Tomorrow," he answered.

"The sooner the better!" exclaimed Bert. "That circus will keep moving on and we don't want it to get too far away with Waggo."

"We might never get him back," sighed

Nan who had become very fond of the dog.

"Poor Waggo!" murmured Flossie.

"I'll make them give him back to us!" declared Freddie.

"Well then, it's all settled," said Mr. Bobbsey. "That's why I said 'All aboard' when I heard what had happened. I thought of the circus as a place where Waggo might be, though I don't yet admit that he was really stolen. He might have wanted to be with the other dogs or even with the elephants."

"It will be fun to see the circus again," Bert said.

"Oh, you won't want to see the circus, will you?" his father asked, winking one eye at his wife. "Why, you just saw it a few days ago and it hasn't changed any."

"Sure we want to see the circus again!" declared Bert. "Why, we'll have to go see it to find out if Professor Mungo has Waggo."

"Well, yes, I suppose so," agreed Mr. Bobbsey. "Anyway, we'll see about it. So get ready for the auto trip. All aboard!" he called again like the conductor of a train or the captain of a boat.

"Oh, what fun we'll have, traveling along!" murmured Nan. "But Mother, I wish you were coming."

"I just can't, Nan, dear. You'll have to take my place and be a mother to Flossie. You once kept house, you know."

"Oh, yes," and Nan smiled, "the time Mrs. Pry tried to help us and got sick herself."

"The poor old lady was so deaf," remarked Bert, "that if Freddie asked her for a piece of bread she would get a rag and tie up his head, thinking he meant he was hurt."

"But we had some fun, for all that," went on Nan. "And we'll have some fun again, following the circus."

"Lots of fun!" Bert agreed. "How long shall we be away, Dad?"

"Oh, a couple of days, perhaps three, for I may have to go farther than Deepdell. So you had better take a change of clothes."

"I'll pack the suitcases," promised Nan.

The Bobbsey twins were so excited that evening, after having heard of their father's plans, that they did not want to go to bed. They preferred to sit up and talk about the adventures they might have and about the chances of getting back the missing Waggo.

At length Mrs. Bobbsey prevailed on Flossie and Freddie to go to their rooms, though after reaching them the small twins called back and forth to each other across the hall.

Bert and Nan were almost as greatly excited and pleased at the prospect of fun ahead of them. They, too, talked back and forth after going to their rooms, some time after Flossie and Freddie had retired. At last their mother was forced to say to them:

"If you don't quiet down and go to sleep, I won't let you go tomorrow!"

This was enough of a threat to silence the older twins. They still could not keep from thinking, in the silence of their rooms, of the joys of the coming trip.

"Maybe," mused Bert, "if Professor Mungo has Waggo he'll teach our dog a lot of tricks before he has to give him back to us."

As for Nan, she was thinking:

"I wonder if I'll be able to look after Flossie? I'll have to manage Freddie, too, for Bert won't do it."

Finally all the twins fell asleep and quiet

settled over the Bobbsey home. Out in the yard Snap, the old dog, wandered from his kennel now and then and came out to look at the moon and whine softly. Perhaps he, too, missed the lost Waggo.

Bright and early the next morning the Bobbsey twins were up to get ready to follow the circus. Bags had been filled with extra clothes, some lunch had been packed, though for the main meals Mr. Bobbsey said he would stop at restaurants along the way. At night he and the children would stop at a hotel.

Nan made one last appeal to her mother to come along but Mrs. Bobbsey said she could not do it.

"You'll have to be a little mother, Nan," she said with a smile.

"All aboard!" called Mr. Bobbsey again as he took his place at the steering wheel of his big car. "All aboard!"

The children piled in, calling last good-byes to their mother, to Dinah, Sam and their pets.

"We'll bring Waggo back!" shouted Bert, little dreaming of what strange adventures were to happen before he was to see his dog again.

"Goodbye and good luck!" called Mrs. Bobbsey.

Then the Bobbsey twins started to follow the circus.

CHAPTER XVIII

A BREAKDOWN

"Isn't this fine!" exclaimed Nan.

"Just dandy!" agreed Bert.

He and his sister sat in the back seat of the big touring car. Just ahead of them on a sort of folding seat, or at least a seat that at times could be pushed back out of the way, sat Freddie. Flossie was in the front with her father. The two small twins had agreed to take turns riding in this place of honor. The space in front of the feet of Nan and Bert was filled with the valises.

"We couldn't have had a better day," went on Nan.

"Regular circus weather," Bert said. "I hope we soon catch up to that show."

"And get Waggo," added Nan.

"Oh, sure!"

The traveling twins and their father were several miles outside of Lakeport by this time. Mr. Bobbsey had made an early morning start and had driven rapidly, for the road was a good one and there was little traffic.

Deepdell was about a day's auto journey from Lakeport and Mr. Bobbsey had some lumber business there to which he must attend. He was glad of the chance it gave him to take the children on an outing, and at the same time afford an opportunity to look for the lost dog.

"If it takes too long to find Waggo," remarked Nan as they journeyed onward, "we won't have time to train him and the other animals for our circus."

"It won't take long to get him back once we catch up to the circus," Bert said.

"You must remember," chimed in his father, "that it isn't at all certain that Waggo is with the circus. It's just a chance. Don't be disappointed if, after we locate the show, your dog isn't there."

"I don't see where else he could be," observed Bert.

"He might be in one of many places," Mr. Bobbsey said. "He may be roaming through the woods, far away, a little lost dog. Or he may have been found and taken in by some family living not far from Lakeport. Then, too, he may have joined the circus."

"Wouldn't it be a good thing," suggested Nan, "to ask as we go along if anyone has seen Waggo? He's such a smart dog anybody who once saw him would remember him."

"Yes, we can do that," her father said, "though it would delay us too much to stop at every house we pass. If, for instance, we need to stop to let one of you have a drink of water, then we can inquire."

"I'm thirsty now!" suddenly remarked Freddie.

"You never would have thought of being thirsty if Daddy hadn't spoken of it!" laughed Nan.

"But I *am* thirsty!" declared the little fellow.

"Well, that looks like a good place to stop and get a drink," said Mr. Bobbsey, pointing toward a farmhouse they were approaching. "I wouldn't object, myself, to a little cool water."

"I'll take some, too," Bert said with a laugh, "as long as Freddie started it."

They drew up at the side of the road in

front of the farmhouse. The twins were glad of the chance to get down and "stretch their legs," as Mr. Bobbsey called it. Opening the front gate, Mr. Bobbsey led the four children toward the house.

A pleasant-faced woman, with a little girl about Flossie's age, who was trying to hide behind her mother's skirts, came out onto the porch. She smiled at the children.

"I wonder," began Mr. Bobbsey, "if we could get some water here? I mean for the twins," he added, indicating the four. "My auto isn't thirsty just now."

"Surely they may have all the water they can drink," said the woman with a laugh. "Just sit down on the porch here in the shade, and I'll bring out a pitcher and some glasses. It's a very warm day."

"Indeed it is," agreed Mr. Bobbsey. "But don't let us put you to so much trouble. If there is a pump outside I'll get the water myself."

"It isn't any trouble. Just sit down and I'll bring it to you. Say, how-d'-do to the little girl, can't you, Mabel?" she urged her own child.

"Hello," murmured the farmer's daughter somewhat timidly.

"Hello!" greeted Flossie more boldly. Then Freddie chimed in with:

"I have a toy fire engine and it squirts real water but I didn't bring it with me."

"We've a dog and two cats," added Flossie, "and one cat had kittens at Christmas and it was a big surprise."

"We got another dog, too," Freddie said, "only we haven't him now 'cause he ran away or maybe a circus took him and——"

Suddenly Mabel seemed to lose her shyness at hearing this talk about animal pets. She walked toward the small Bobbsey twins and said:

"I got a dog, too. He's a nice dog and he came to me yesterday. He was walking along the road, all dusty, and I called him in and I gave him a drink of water and he wagged his tail and he licked my hands with his tongue, and my mother says I may keep him."

"What kind of a dog is it?" asked Bert quickly, while he and Nan exchanged glances.

"Maybe it's our dog!" cried Freddie as

Mabel's mother came back on the porch with a tray containing a pitcher of cool, sparkling water with glasses grouped about it.

The hearts of the Bobbsey twins beat high with hope as they heard this news about a stray dog. Mabel seemed a bit frightened at the eagerness of the visitors.

"Did this dog that you say came to you yesterday, along the road, have any spots on him?" asked Bert.

"Have you folks lost a dog?" inquired Mrs. Merkel, which was the name of the farmer's wife.

"Yes," Mr. Bobbsey said. "We didn't exactly *lose* it, for Waggo went off by himself in the night, or else he was taken, perhaps by some of the circus men. We're on our way to Deepdell now, to see if we can find Waggo."

"Maybe he's the dog you say came to you," suggested Nan, but a moment later she felt sorry she had spoken for a sad and disappointed look came over Mabel's face.

"Well, we surely have a stray dog," Mrs. Merkel said as she set the tray on a table and poured out five glasses of water for the thirsty travelers. "My little girl took a notion to him, and as she's rather lonesome here, I said she might keep him. But of course if he's your dog——"

"Oh, it isn't at all certain he is our dog!" Mr. Bobbsey quickly said. "Of course, it *might* be. We'd have to look at him to make sure. Waggo does tricks——"

"This dog does tricks!" impulsively interrupted Mabel, who now seemed to have lost all her shyness. "He shook paws with me."

"Did this dog have any spots on him?" asked Bert again.

Mabel shook her head and at this the hearts of the Bobbsey twins grew sad again.

"No," said the little farm girl, "my dog is just plain. He isn't trimmed with spots. He's brown all over and he has long hair and ears."

"A sort of spaniel," said Mr. Bobbsey. "Then it can't be Waggo, for he was of the terrier variety. I'm glad, for the sake of your little girl," he said to the woman, "that it isn't our dog that came to her. But I'm sorry for my children, who are very fond of their missing pet. We shall have to search farther."

"There's my dog now!" suddenly cried

Mabel. She pointed to a little brown animal that came around the corner of the house, wagging its tail. At sight of it Bert said with a sigh of disappointment:

"That isn't our dog!"

"I'm glad of that," remarked Mrs. Merkel. "I mean, I'm glad for Mabel," she added. "Will you have some more water?"

"Thank you, no," answered Mr. Bobbsey. "That was very good but we have had enough, I think."

"Yes," murmured Nan. "It was lovely. Oh, what a pretty dog!" she exclaimed as the brown animal came closer.

"He wasn't pretty when he wandered in here off the road," said Mrs. Merkel with a laugh. "He was more dust and mud than dog. But he is right pretty when he's cleaned."

"And he loves me and I love him," chimed in Mabel. "See how he shakes paws."

She made her dog do this simple trick. Then, after a little more talk, during which Mrs. Merkel said she had not seen Waggo, the Bobbsey twins traveled on with their father.

It was later in the afternoon, and they were

still some miles from Deepdell, when the auto gave a sudden lurch, tilted to one side, and before Mr. Bobbsey could check it or steer it away, the car had run into a wayside ditch. There it came to a quick stop, leaning over so far that the children were almost spilled out.

"Oh, what happened?" cried Nan, catching hold of Flossie who now sat with her and Bert.

"I guess we've had a breakdown," her father said as he jumped out of the car. "Yes," he added as he looked beneath it, "the steering gear is broken. We can't go any farther!"

"Oh, dear!" sighed Nan.

"Then the circus will go away with Waggo before we can catch up to it!" murmured Bert.

Tears came into the eyes of Flossie and Freddie.

CHAPTER XIX

FREDDIE HEARS SOMETHING

Mr. Bobbsey was walking around the stalled car, looking beneath it, here and there, to see what damage had been done.

"Nothing very much the matter," he said at last. "Only we can't go any farther until the steering gear is mended. We shall have to stay here all night."

"Daddy!" exclaimed Nan in a shocked voice. "Oh!"

"Stay here all night!" cried Bert. "Why, Dad, look at the place!"

They were on a lonely road. On both sides were thick trees and bushes. Ahead and behind the place where the car had come to a stop in the ditch were more trees and bushes.

"It's a very lonesome place to stay all night," went on Nan.

"I think it's fun!" exclaimed Freddie.

"So do I," echoed Flossie. "We can stay in the woods and have a picnic."

By this time Mr. Bobbsey had finished looking at the broken part of his car so he could pay more attention to what the children were saying. Not until Nan spoke about it being such a lonesome place to spend the night did the father of the twins realize that this was so.

"You're right, Nan!" he said. "We can't stay here. I wasn't thinking of what I said. I expected we would get to the next town, even if we could not make Deepdell where the circus is, and we could stay at a hotel. But now—" he shook his head in a puzzled way.

"I think it'll be more fun to stay here than at a hotel," said Freddie.

"Heaps and heaps!" added Flossie.

"Oh, but we haven't any place to sleep, objected Nan.

"We haven't much to eat," spoke Bert, looking at the boxes and basket that had held some sandwiches and cake. "We ate most of it up on the road and we'll be wanting supper pretty soon and breakfast in the morning."

"That's so," agreed his father.

"I'm sort of hungry now," said Freddie.

"So'm I!" sighed his little twin sister.

"Well," went on Mr. Bobbsey, "there's no getting away from the fact that we can't go any farther until the car is mended. I shall have to find a garage. Also, it's very true that we can't stay here in the woods, with night coming on. If we had the big sedan I might manage to let you twins sleep in it, and perhaps I could go hunting and find something to eat. But in the open car, and with the nights as cool as they have been lately, it's out of the question."

"Then what are we going to do?" asked Nan, thinking of what her mother had said —that she must look after Flossie and Freddie.

"We'll have to walk to the nearest town," decided Bert. "There may be a hotel there."

"It's a long way to the next town, as I remember the road map," said Mr. Bobbsey. "The best thing to do, I think, would be to find a house where we might stay all night and where we could get something to eat. That's what we'll do, look for a house."

"The last house we passed, just before we had this accident," Bert remarked, "is a long way back. I remember it—a big white house and a red barn."

"It was a lovely place," Nan said.

"That would have been a good place to have had our accident happen," said the twins's father. "As it didn't, and as we must stay some place I think the best thing to do will be for one of us to walk ahead, down this road, until a house is found. Maybe they'll have a car and they'll come and get Flossie and Freddie, if they can't take all of us. You and I, Bert," his father said, "could manage to camp out in the auto, if there isn't room for us all at the house we may find. Nan, Flossie and Freddie must be under shelter."

"Oh, I want to camp out!" Freddie cried.

"So do I!" chimed in Flossie.

"No, you must stay with me and do as Daddy says," suggested Nan.

"I'll go down the road and try to find a house where we can all stay," offered Bert. "If I see a garage I'll ask the man to come and fix the car."

"You aren't likely to find a garage in such a lonesome place as this," Mr. Bobbsey declared. "Maybe, if you locate a house, they could telephone for a mechanic. All right, Bert. Start your exploration and see if you can help us out. I'll stay here with Nan, Flossie and Freddie."

"I'll hurry," Bert said as he started off on a fast walk. "It will soon be dark."

"Yes do," urged his father. "But don't tire yourself. There is about an hour of twilight left. I should not have come by this lonesome road, but it was a short cut and I wanted to reach Deepdell before night."

"Do you think the circus will move on and take Waggo?" asked Flossie anxiously.

"If they go away we'll keep after 'em!" declared Freddie.

"Oh, I think we'll catch up to the circus all right," Mr. Bobbsey answered. "But there is no way of being sure they have your dog. It may be we are on what is called a wild goose chase."

"Why are you going to chase a wild goose?" asked Flossie, as Bert disappeared around a bend in the road.

Her father laughed as he answered:

"I'm not going to chase any wild goose. That's just a saying which means you are after something that is hard to find. You see, we aren't at all sure that the circus man took your dog. But as long as I had to go to Deep-dell anyhow, it was just as well to follow the circus."

"I'm sure Waggo is in the circus," Flossie said.

Mr. Bobbsey was looking along the road for a spring of water, as the small twins had said, more than once, that they were again thirsty, and Nan was getting together what food remained in the pasteboard boxes and the basket, trying to calculate how to make it do for supper and breakfast if she had to, when there was a shout down the road and Freddie called:

"Here comes Bert!"

"Sure enough!" echoed Mr. Bobbsey who just then had located a little spring of sparkling water beside the road. "What luck, Bert?" he asked, as the boy came running toward the stalled auto.

"Good luck!" Bert answered.

"Did you find a hotel?" called Nan.

"No," her brother replied, "but I found a farmhouse and we can stay there all night.

They have a telephone, and there's a garage in the next town, about five miles from here, so I guess everything will be all right."

"Good boy! Fine!" his father said. "Now we'll start and walk to this farmhouse. Bert, I guess you and I will have to carry the baggage. If it isn't far we can make two trips."

"It isn't far," Bert said. "The house is just around the next bend. But we won't have to walk."

"Why?" Nan wanted to know.

"Because the farmer is coming to get us in his car. He's a nice man."

"An *ice man!*" exclaimed Freddie. "I thought you said he was a *farmer.*"

"Oh, I see what you mean. I talked too fast," chuckled Bert. "Well, he is *a—nice—* man," and he separated the words. "He is a nice farmer."

"That's hard to say when you're in a hurry," remarked Nan. "But I'm glad we don't have to stay here all night."

"It wouldn't be very jolly," Bert said. "I was lucky to find the house so near."

"I hope all our bad luck ended when the steering gear broke," said Mr. Bobbsey. "And

I'm glad my little fireman and my fat fairy do not have to walk far to get shelter. Ah, I guess this is the farmer coming now."

A rattling auto appeared around the bend, following close after Bert, and soon the Bobbseys and their baggage were safe in the old farmhouse where Jacob Powden lived with his wife. They were an elderly couple who made Mr. Bobbsey and the children welcome.

After Mr. Bobbsey had telephoned to the garage and a man had promised to come out and tow the stalled car in to repair it, the travelers had time to look about them. They were glad to be in such a comfortable place for the night. Of course, Flossie and Freddie told about the search for the dog, mentioning that they were following the circus to get Waggo back.

"I'm afraid you'll be disappointed again," Mr. Powden said.

"Why?" asked Bert.

"Well, I heard that the circus isn't coming to Deepdell after all. It was to be there to-day and tomorrow, but it didn't arrive. I sell farm stuff in Deepdell and I was there this forenoon. There was no circus then and a lot of folks said it was going to some other place instead."

"Oh!" exclaimed Bert.

"That's too bad!" echoed Nan.

"But where is the circus?" asked Flossie.

"And where's our dog?" Freddie wanted to know.

"That I can't tell you," answered the farmer. "I dare say the circus made a change in its plans. You ought to be able to find it, though."

"I think we shall," spoke Mr. Bobbsey. "I'll make inquiries when I get to Deepdell. I have to go there, anyhow."

In spite of what their father said about being sure he could find the missing circus later, Flossie and Freddie were a bit worried. Nan and Bert did not feel any too happy when they thought of their missing dog, either. A little later, however, they were all quite jolly as they sat about the table to eat the fine supper Mrs. Powden put on the table. The evening was spent in sitting out on the porch until it was time to go to bed.

Flossie and Nan had a room for themselves, as did Bert and Freddie. Mr. Bobbsey was in a room next to the boys. Nan and her sister were soon asleep, but Freddie insisted on staying awake to talk to Bert about the chances of getting Waggo back, until at last Bert said:

"You go to sleep, Freddie, or Dad will come in here to see why you are staying awake so late. Go to sleep!"

"All right," answered the little fellow. He lapsed into silence and Bert fell asleep. He was awakened some time later in the night, however, by hearing his small brother loudly whispering:

"Bert! Bert! I hear something!"

"What do you hear, Freddie?"

"I don't know, but I think it's a bear trying to get in our room. Where's your flashlight?"

As Bert fumbled for it beneath his pillow, he also heard a strange noise in the dark room.

CHAPTER XX

ON THE TRAIL AGAIN

"THERE it is!" cried Freddie.

Bert switched on his light and sent the flashing beam into the corners of the room.

"Where?" he asked. "Where did you see the bear, Freddie?"

"I didn't *see* it," was the answer. "I just *heard* it! There, I heard it again!"

There was a noise in the corner of the room by the bureau. Bert also heard it and flashed the light in that direction.

"I'm not sure it's a bear," Freddie said.

"Of course it isn't a bear!" spoke Bert. "How would a bear get into the house?"

"I don't know," Freddie replied. "Maybe it climbed up the rain-water pipe."

"A bear couldn't do that," Bert declared. "A bear, to climb, has to have something he can stick his claws in, like a telegraph pole or the trunk of a tree."

"Well," resumed Freddie as Bert continued to flash the light, endeavoring to see what was making the noise, "anyhow, there's a tree just outside our window. I saw it when I was getting ready for bed. Maybe the bear climbed up that."

"There isn't any bear, I tell you!" whispered Bert, not wanting to awaken his father in the next room by loud talking.

"Well, it's something!" declared Freddie. "There, I heard the noise again and it's a loud noise."

This was indeed true. Bert heard a clatter and bang, a loud sound, and it was certain that something, or some one besides the two boys, was in the room.

Suddenly a loud "Meow!" was heard, and Freddie and Bert laughed together as they exclaimed:

"A cat!"

A moment later a pussy came from the corner near the bureau. She was clearly seen in the gleam of Bert's flashlight; but no sooner had Freddie caught sight of pussy than he cried:

"What's on its head?"

"One of my shoes!" exclaimed Bert with a

laugh. "That's what made the thumping noise. The cat got its head in my shoe and couldn't get it out. I guess the poor thing's scared. I'll take the shoe off."

Bert jumped out of bed and ran around the room after the cat, who was uttering sad "meows" and seemed much frightened. Bert got the little animal into a corner at last, however, and pulled off the shoe. Then the pussy purred happily and let Bert and Freddie pet it.

"What's going on in there?" asked Mr. Bobbsey, who by this time had been awakened by the commotion.

"It's just a cat that got into our room and tried to wear one of my shoes on its head," Bert answered.

"I thought it was a bear," Freddie said, as the cat with a final purr went out of the door into the dark hall.

"Are you boys playing some game?" Mr. Bobbsey asked, wanting to laugh but not thinking it wise just then.

"Oh no, Dad, there really was a cat," Bert explained. "I guess it was just snooping around when it happened to get its head stuck in my shoe. Then the cat thumped it on the floor and Freddie thought it was a bear."

"I don't think so now and I'm going to bed," said the little fellow.

"Yes, it's time," agreed Mr. Bobbsey with a chuckle beneath the bedclothes, as he thought of how funny a cat would look with a shoe on its head.

"I'll fix it so pussy won't get in again," Bert said as he closed the bedroom door. He and his little brother were not further disturbed that night.

Flossie and Freddie had slept well. Around the breakfast table in the morning the Bobbsey family talked over their plans. By telephone Mr. Bobbsey learned from the garage that his car would be ready about ten o'clock, a mechanic having worked on it during the night. It would be driven to the farmhouse and the travelers could get in and resume their journey.

"Then we'll follow the circus," Bert said.

"We don't know where it is," Nan reminded him. "If it didn't go to Deepdell, where did it go?"

"That's what we must find out," said Bert.

The children, while waiting for the car to come from the village garage, petted the pussy which had so startled Freddie. She was a friendly cat.

"Almost as nice as our Snoop and the Christmas pussy," Flossie declared.

"Have you a dog?" Freddie asked the farmer.

"No, we haven't a dog," Mr. Powden replied. "I've been calculatin' to get one for quite a spell but I never get around to it."

"We have two dogs, only we haven't one of 'em now," said Freddie. "But we're after him. If we can find the circus maybe we can find Waggo."

"I hope you do," the farmer said.

When the repaired auto came to the farmhouse the Bobbseys got in with their baggage, and after bidding Mr. Powden and his wife goodbye, after thanking them for their kindness, the travelers once more started for Deepdell.

The journey into the small city did not take long, and the travelers reached it before noon. Though they had looked for some sign of a circus on the way, they saw none.

"I guess it turned off to another place," Mr. Bobbsey said.

He was driving down the main street, on his way to the office of the man with whom he had to do some business, when all of a sudden there was a clatter and bang, the tooting of whistles and the ringing of bells.

"Oh, it's a fire! A fire!" cried Freddie. "The engines are coming! Maybe the circus is on fire!"

CHAPTER XXI

FLOSSIE IS HUNGRY

THERE certainly was a fire; at least, the engines were coming to answer an alarm.

"The circus can't be on fire!" exclaimed Bert.

"Of course it can't, Freddie!" chimed in Nan. "For there isn't any circus here to burn."

"That's so," agreed Freddie. "Anyhow, here comes the puffer!" He often called a fire engine a "puffer," even though in this day most fire engines work by gasoline pumps and not by steam ones. The "puffer" did, indeed, come dashing by at that moment, Mr. Bobbsey having pulled over to the curb, as did many other drivers, to allow the fire apparatus to go past.

"Go on, Daddy! Follow it!" begged Freddie. "Let's see where the fire is!"

"Don't go too close!" begged Flossie. "We don't want to catch fire ourselves."

"Indeed we don't!" agreed her father, looking to see if the way was clear before turning back toward the middle of the street.

"If any sparks from the fire catch on us I'll put 'em out with my fire engine that squirts real water," Freddie declared. Then, as he happened to remember something he said a little sadly, "Oh, no, I can't! My engine's home!"

"Don't worry! I'm not going close enough to get in any danger," Mr. Bobbsey remarked. "I don't believe in chasing after fire engines. There's excitement enough in the streets without automobiles adding to it."

However, to please the children, he went as near the scene of the blaze as he thought was safe. There was a great deal of noise and excitement, but the fire did not amount to much. It was in an old building on a side street and the flames were soon put out. Then the crowds began scattering, the hundreds of autos rolled away and the fire engines and the hook and ladder trucks went back to their quarters.

"I don't call that much of a fire," grumbled Freddie when it was all over. "I've seen lots bigger ones than that right in Lakeport."

"I guess the firemen and the owner of the property are glad the blaze was no worse," Mr. Bobbsey remarked. "Fires are not things to be wished for."

"I thought our house was on fire once," remarked Nan.

"I remember that," Bert said with a laugh. "It was when we were keeping house and we had poor, old Mrs. Pry to help us. It was just some smoke, though, wasn't it, Nan?"

"Just smoke, that's all. I was glad it wasn't a fire. Oh, what a time we had then!"

"Yes, I guess you did," her father remarked. "Well, now that the fire is over and it is pretty certain that the circus isn't coming to Deepdell, I must attend to my business. As I can't very well take you children along I must find a place where I can leave you."

"Leave us, Daddy!" gasped Flossie. "Are you going away and leave us all alone?"

"Just for a little while. But you won't be alone, for all you twins will be together. Nan will look after you and Freddie and Bert can look after himself. I think."

"Sure!" murmured Bert the older Bobbsey boy.

"I am going to take you to a hotel," went on Mr. Bobbsey. "We shall stay in Deepdell over night, perhaps for two nights if I don't finish my business. Before I go to see Mr. Layton about a lot of lumber he wants to buy from me, I'll take you to the hotel."

"I think it's lots of fun to live at a hotel," remarked Nan.

"So do I," agreed Bert, "but I hope we get enough to eat."

"You will," his father chuckled.

"Will they let us have any fun in the hotel?" Freddie wanted to know.

"Some kinds of fun," Nan answered, for she remembered several occasions when she and her mother had stopped at one of these places.

"May we play tag?" Flossie went on.

"If you don't make too much noise running about the halls and rooms," Nan replied. "You must not disturb the other guests."

"We'll play whisper tag," proposed Flossie.

"Sure!" assented Freddie. This was a quiet

form of the game which he and his twin sister had arranged for themselves to play on the days when they had to stay in, and their mother, perhaps, had a headache.

Mr. Bobbsey had been in Deepdell several times before this visit, so he knew his way around the small city. His first care was to get the twins settled in a hotel. There were two such places in Deepdell. Mr. Bobbsey picked out the smaller hotel where he and his wife had stopped more than once, but where the children had never stayed.

The clerk greeted the lumber merchant as he walked into the lobby, followed by the two sets of twins, and then remarked:

"So you brought the family with you this time, Mr. Bobbsey."

"Not all the family," was the laughing answer. "I left a good part of it at home—my wife. But this is the liveliest part," he chuckled, indicating Nan and the others. "Especially these two," and he touched Flossie and Freddie lightly on their blond heads.

"I expect so," agreed the clerk. "Well, we're glad to have you with us. Now I'll see what I can do for you."

"I'm going to sleep with Bert!" spoke Freddie Bobbsey.

"And I'm going to sleep with Nan!" chimed in Flossie.

"Well, that means two rooms and another for you, Mr. Bobbsey," went on the clerk. "I guess we can fix you up. We have plenty of room."

"I guess you wouldn't have had if the circus had come to town," spoke the lumber merchant.

"No, that's right. But the circus disappointed us. I heard they had some sort of accident and couldn't make Deepdell. They went to Greenberg, I hear."

"It rather spoils my plans," said Mr. Bobbsey. "I brought the children here to see the circus."

"My stars!" exclaimed the clerk, who was an old friend of Mr. Bobbsey, "you don't mean to say you came all the way over from Lakeport to our city to see the circus? Why, I understood it showed in your town."

"Yes, it did, for several days," Mr. Bobbsey said. "But my children have a trick dog and it disappeared when the circus left town.

They have an idea that a dog trainer in the show might have taken away their pet. As I had to come here on business, I brought the twins along so they could look over the circus and perhaps find Waggo."

"That's too bad, to have a pet dog gone!" sympathized the hotel clerk. "I hope you get him back."

"Have you a trained dog that will climb a ladder?" asked Freddie while Mr. Bobbsey was signing the register book.

"No, little man, I haven't a dog of any kind, or a cat, either," went on Mr. Blunton. "I have one pet I think a lot of, but——"

He did not have time to say more just then, as other guests came in and he had to attend to them. A colored bell-boy took the Bobbsey baggage up on an elevator, and showed the travelers their rooms. Flossie and Freddie greatly enjoyed the little trip in the "lift," as our English friends call the elevator.

"I like it!" chuckled Flossie.

"So do I," added Freddie. "It makes you feel so funny in the middle of your stomach when the elevator stops all of a sudden."

Nan and Flossie were shown into a pleasant room which had a bathroom adjoining, at the front of the hotel. Bert and Freddie had a room next to the one where their father would sleep, the two being connected by a bathroom.

"And now," said Mr. Bobbsey when they were partly settled, "I'll have luncheon with you and then I'll leave you to yourselves until late in the afternoon. I'll be here in time for supper, though. Please don't any of you get lost!" he advised, as they seated themselves at the table.

"We won't," Nan said.

The children felt a little lonely, when later their father went away to see Mr. Layton about some lumber. However, the small twins brightened up when Nan and Bert discovered that in the very hotel where they were stopping there would be shown that afternoon some moving pictures, especially interesting to children. The hotel clerk told Nan about the show and said he would have one of his housekeepers bring the twins into the auditorium and get them good seats.

The picture was one the children had no

seen before and they enjoyed it very much, even though, because of the small machine that had to be used, it was not a "talkie."

"It's kind of nice to be quiet once in a while," remarked Nan. The picture was funny, so Freddie and Flossie did not miss the talk because they laughed so much.

Coming out of the show about four o'clock, Flossie, wandering around the hotel lobby, suddenly remarked:

"I'm hungry! I'm going to get something to eat. I can't wait for supper."

"I can't, either," said Freddie. "Let's go find some food."

At that moment Bert and Nan were standing near the news-stand at one side of the lobby, looking for a magazine they might buy to read. At that moment they were not paying attention to the small twins. When Nan turned around, she missed both Flossie and Freddie and at once exclaimed:

"Oh, Bert! Where are they?"

"That's so! They've disappeared!" Bert said, seeing neither of the small twins, "but I guess they can't be far away. They may have gone up in the elevator to our rooms. They're crazy about riding in it."

"Oh, I hope they are up there and haven't wandered out in the street and got lost!" exclaimed Nan. "I shouldn't have taken my eyes away from them!"

"That's right. You must watch 'em every second!" Bert agreed. "I think they're up in the rooms. Let's go look."

Flossie and Freddie were not there. Descending to the lobby again, Bert and Nan began an anxious search.

Meanwhile, the little twins were having an adventure all by themselves.

CHAPTER XXII

PROFESSOR MUNGO'S DOGS

FLOSSIE and Freddie, having turned away from Bert and Nan at the newspaper stand, walked toward the dining room of the hotel. At this hour of the day, shortly before five o'clock, this room was not open for meals. The doors were not locked, though, and the twins made their way inside, looking at the rows of chairs and at the small tables, already covered with white cloths, and set for dinner.

"When I grow up I'm going to have a dining room just like this," said Flossie, who admired it very much. "There's such a lot of room in it, Freddie."

"Yes," he agreed. "Nobody would bump into anybody else. Oh, there's the way to the kitchen," he added, pointing to a green door out of which he and his sister had seen the waiters coming with big trays heaped with dishes and food.

"I hope they'll give us something to eat!"

"Sure they will," declared Freddie. "I have the money to pay for it," and he took a nickel and a dime from his pocket.

"That won't buy much," Flossie said with a sigh.

The twins pushed through the swinging doors. Freddie was right. They led into the hotel kitchen, where in front of big stoves several white-aproned and white-capped men were busy preparing for the rush that always accompanies a meal hour in a hotel.

One of the cooks, seeing the children, gave a start of surprise. He said something to another cook and then walked toward Flossie and Freddie.

"We came to get something to eat. I'm hungry!" Flossie explained before the cooks had a chance to answer a question.

"We have the money to pay for it," Freddie went on, taking out the dime and the nickel.

The two cooks smiled, then they laughed aloud. Another man, rather dignified, who was dressed all in black except that his shirt, of which a good deal showed, was very white and gleaming, came toward the twins.

"What is it?" he asked, and Freddie and Flossie knew him to be the head waiter who had talked with their father.

"I'm hungry!" Flossie announced.

"We want fifteen cents worth of food," said Freddie. "Here's your money."

For a moment the head waiter did not seem to know what to do; neither did the white-uniformed cooks. Then the head waiter laughed and said:

"Oh, now I know who they are! The small half of the Bobbsey twins. All right, my little friends," he went on, still laughing, "you shall have something to eat and I'll charge it to your father's bill. I can't serve you in the main dining room as it isn't open yet. However, you may come into the dining room where I eat."

"We don't mind where it is, as long as we get something to eat," said Flossie. "Thank you," she added, as an afterthought.

"Yes, thank you," murmured Freddie.

"Come this way," invited the head waiter, and he led them to a small dining room off the kitchen, where several waiters and wait-resses were having their early supper so they would be ready to serve the hotel guests. Freddie and Flossie were seated at a small table, and one of the waitresses smilingly brought them some food—two glasses of milk, some sandwiches and cookies.

"You'd better not eat too much or you won't have any appetites for your regular supper," she said.

"Oh, I never can eat too much," Freddie declared.

"Me either," added Flossie, wishing to keep up with her brother.

Thus it was at their own private meal that Flossie and Freddie were found, a little later, by Nan and Bert. The older twins told of the missing ones to the hotel clerk, and a search was at once started. Of course, the lost two were soon located, much to Nan's and Bert's relief.

"Why did you ever do a thing like this?" asked Nan, who was much shocked by the escapade, as she called it.

"We were hungry, weren't we, Freddie?" asked Flossie, swallowing the last of a cookie.

"Sure!" was the answer. "But I'm not so hungry now."

"I shouldn't think you would be," remarked Bert with a laugh.

"I hope Waggo had, as good a meal as we did," Flossie said as she and Freddie followed Nan and Bert back to the lobby.

"Oh yes, poor Waggo! I wonder where he is?" Freddie sighed.

"We certainly are chasing around the country after him," remarked Bert. "We came to Deepdell and next we're going to Greenberg. If we don't catch up to the circus there I wonder where we'll go next?"

"I'm afraid Daddy won't take us much farther if we don't get Waggo back in Greenberg," spoke Nan. "We can't expect him to spend a lot of time driving around after a dog."

"Oh, but we have to get Waggo back!" cried Flossie.

"We can't have our circus without him," said Freddie.

"I'd like to get him back myself," declared Bert, "but it isn't going to be easy."

Mr. Bobbsey laughed over the adventures of Flossie and Freddie when he joined the children at supper. The small twins seemed to enjoy the meal as much as did Nan and Bert, in spite of the extra refreshments the two explorers had taken.

"My little fireman and my fat fairy certainly know how to get what they want," Mr. Bobbsey said as he pinched Flossie's cheek.

"But what about Waggo, Dad?" asked Bert.

"Do you think we'll ever get him?"

"I hope so," was the answer, though Mr. Bobbsey in his heart did not believe there was much chance of finding the missing dog. "At any rate," he added, "we'll stop in Greenberg and see the circus, that is, if it's there and hasn't turned off on some other route. We can go back to Lakeport by way of Greenberg as well as any other way. We'll be there day after tomorrow."

Part of the next day was used by Mr. Bobbsey in attending to some of his business. In the evening he took the children to a show and early the next day they started for Greenberg. Mr. Bobbsey had learned by telephone that the circus had finally reached that city.

"Maybe we'll find Waggo now!" exclaimed

Flossie when they were once more in the auto traveling onward.

"I guess he'll be glad to see us!" echoed Freddie.

"Poor dog!" murmured Nan. "I hope he has been well cared for and has had enough to eat."

"Oh," said Bert, "whoever has Waggo will take good care of him, I'm sure. He's such a valuable dog nobody would let him go hungry. If Professor Mungo has him we'll take him away."

Mr. Bobbsey drove his car fast and reached Greenberg before noon. He went at once to a hotel, for he had decided to remain over night and start back for Lakeport in the morning.

"That," he said, "will give us time to look in the circus for Waggo."

That the circus was in town was soon evident, for all about were the gay bills and posters telling about it. After luncheon Mr. Bobbsey took the children out to the grounds. They saw the same tents, gay with fluttering flags and banners, and after buying tickets they pushed their way into the side-show tent. If Waggo were anywhere with the circus, Mr.

Bobbsey said, he would be with Professor Mungo's collection of trick dogs. So it was with anxious and fast-beating hearts that the Bobbsey twins hurried toward the platform, where once before they had seen the "marvelous performing canines."

"This way, Ladies and Gents! This way!" cried the side-show announcer, just as he had done at Lakeport. "This way to witness the most wonderful and marvelous aggregation of almost human canines ever before gathered under canvas! This way! This way!"

A whining and barking could be heard. Professor Mungo was coming up the back steps leading to his platform, his performing dogs following him.

Would Waggo be among them?

The answer to this question was eagerly awaited by each Bobbsey twin.

CHAPTER XXIII

WHINING, yapping, barking and leaping about in excitement, as if eager to begin their performance, Professor Mungo's dogs scurried around him as he walked around the platform and began to arrange the ladders, the big hoops and other things used in the performing of tricks. Freddie and Flossie had pushed themselves up into the front row of spectators in order to be able to see better, while Nan and Bert, their father near them, were just back of the small twins.

One look at the collection of dogs which the trainer had brought up on the platform with him was enough to disclose that Waggo was not among them.

"He isn't here!" whispered Flossie in disappointed tones.

"No, Waggo isn't there!" agreed Freddie and his voice, too, was sad. "But maybe he's keeping him hid so we won't see him."

"These aren't all the dogs," said Bert in a low voice.

"What do you mean?"

"Well," Bert resumed, "don't you remember, Professor Mungo has two parts to his dog act? This is the first part where a lot of dogs all do about the same things. In the second part he brings out some more dogs and they do the ambulance act."

"Oh, yes!" agreed Nan.

"Well," said Bert, "maybe he has Waggo in that part of the show. We'll wait and see."

"Surely!" murmured Nan. She whispered this news to Flossie and Freddie and the small twins took heart again. Eagerly they watched the dogs perform. They had seen it all before, but they did not tire of viewing it again. However, they were eager for the second part of the performance. Then, perhaps, they might see Waggo.

It did not take Professor Mungo long to hurry through the first part of his dog act. The more often crowds can be hurried into and out of side-shows the more money can be made. Nothing lasts very long in a side-show. In a few minutes the "Professor," looking at the crowd in front of his platform, announced:

"I will now show you some marvelous tricks my dogs can do!"

Professor Mungo did not seem to recognize the Bobbsey twins though all four were close to him. First he sent some of the dogs off the platform to their kennels underneath and in the rear. Then he called to a helper who sent up the animals that were to perform in the ambulance trick. As the dogs started with their parts, drawing the clanging ambulance, Freddie looked at one of the animals and then loudly cried:

"There's our Waggo!"

"Yes, there he is!" shouted Flossie.

"I believe they're right!" said Bert in a low voice.

"It looks like him!" said Nan.

Freddie and Flossie were now so excitedly calling and shouting, meanwhile dancing up and down and begging Waggo to come to them, that the performance came to a stop. Professor Mungo looked down over the edge of his platform straight at Flossie and Freddie, and demanded:

"What's the matter? What are you shouting about?"

"You have our dog!" said Freddie boldly.

"Our trick Waggo! There he is!" exclaimed Flossie, pointing at one of the performing canines.

"Nonsense!" blustered the circus man. "I haven't your dog! These are all mine. You are stopping my show! Please be quiet!"

But Flossie and Freddie cried together:

"We want our dog!"

By this time there was so much excitement in the side-show tent that the manager came hurrying up as fast as he could run.

"What's all this?" he demanded of the children. Then as he saw that they were with Mr. Bobbsey, he went on, "What's the matter, Sir?"

"My twins think your man has their trick dog Waggo," said Mr. Bobbsey. "I must say he looks very much like the animal that disappeared from my house the night your show left Lakeport."

"This is my dog!" declared the "Professor."

"Can you prove it?" asked Mr. Bobbsey.

"I certainly can! Why should I take your dog?"

"Because," said Bert, stepping up, "you wanted to buy Waggo as he was such a good trick dog. When we wouldn't sell him to you, you said we'd be sorry. Then the circus left and our dog was missing. The one you have is our dog—anyhow, he looks and acts like him," Bert declared.

"Oh, now I know who you are!" exclaimed Professor Mungo. "The Bobbsey twins, of course! I didn't know you at first. Well yes, I did want to buy your trick dog," he admitted, "and I was sorry when you would not sell him to me to take the place of my dog who died. But I didn't take your dog. I wouldn't do such a thing. It is true I have a new trick dog in place of the one that died, and he does look like your Waggo at a distance. But I can prove by several men in this circus that I bought this dog the day after we left Lakeport. Here, take a good look at him and you'll see though he is *somewhat* like your Waggo there is a *difference*. Take a look, Mr. Bobbsey," he invited. "I'm not trying to fool you."

Though Flossie and Freddie were still quite

sure that the trick circus dog they now saw was their missing Waggo, Bert and Mr. Bobbsey knew, as they looked at the animal more closely, that it was differently colored and formed.

"No, this isn't Waggo," Mr. Bobbsey had to admit after he had carefully examined the new trick dog.

"If he were Waggo he would know me," Bert said. "This dog is friendly enough, but not as friendly as Waggo would be."

Flossie and Freddie hated to admit that it was not Waggo. Yet even they had to agree, after Freddie tried the circus dog with a little trick of sitting up and holding a piece of candy on his nose, that they had made a mistake. Freddie had taught Waggo to do this, at a word of command snapping the candy up into the air and catching it in his mouth. The circus dog could not do this.

"Oh, dear! He isn't Waggo!" Flossie sighed unhappily. "But where is Waggo?"

No one could answer this. Professor Mungo said he was sorry, for he, too, was a lover of dogs, and knew just how bad owners, especially children, feel when their pet is missing.

"I shouldn't dream of taking your dog," said the trainer to the children, as he got ready to go on with the act. "I admit it might have sounded to you as though I was going to take him, the night I saw you on the circus grounds when we were leaving," the man said to Bert. "But I only meant, if you wanted to sell that dog, I would give you a good price for him. I had to have another dog and I bought this one."

"Yes, I see," Bert admitted.

The side-show went on and after the dog act Professor Mungo invited the Bobbseys into his own little private tent, back of his platform, where they made friends with all the trained dogs. Some circus men told how they had been with Professor Mungo when he bought the new trick dog, after the show had left Lakeport.

"Well, that ends it," said Mr. Bobbsey as they came from the side-show tent. "We'll have to go back to Lakeport without Waggo."

The twins felt so sad that their father took them to the main performance of the circus again to cheer them up before going back to the hotel. They also went through the animal tent and hurried to the space where the elephants were chained.

"There's Hamba!" cried Freddie.

"Well, don't feed him any more handbags!"

"We'll get him some peanuts!" offered Flossie, and this they did.

"Ho! The Bobbsey twins again!" cried Bill Button, the elephant keeper. "I'm glad to see you and so is Hamba—*Salute!*" he ordered, and the elephant raised his trunk high in the air.

The twins greatly enjoyed being among the animals again and it seemed that Hamba was glad to see them. At any rate, his small eyes twinkled as he took a bag of peanuts from Freddie and another from Flossie.

"Hamba just loves children!" said Bill Button with a laugh.

"I guess he loves peanuts, too!" laughed Nan.

"Well yes, a little!" the keeper admitted, smiling.

In spite of not finding Waggo with the circus, the Bobbsey twins enjoyed the performance in the "big top," even though they had seen all the acts before. Yet when in the "grand concert" Professor Mungo showed off his dogs, Nan thought she saw a tear in Flossie's eyes as the little girl watched. She was thinking of the lost Waggo.

It was rather a sad party of children which started back to Lakeport the next day in the auto.

"Do you think we'll ever find our dog, Daddy?" asked Freddie as he sat with his father in the front seat.

"Well, you never can tell," was the answer. "Strange things sometimes happen. We have another night and a day on the road. Maybe we'll find Waggo yet."

Flossie and Freddie felt new hope in their hearts, but Bert and Nan had about given up. However, they did not say this to the small twins. On and on they all journeyed. Mr. Bobbsey expected to stop for the night in the city of Highfield. He was driving along a country road which in a short time would lead into the main highway that would take him to Highfield, when suddenly a man came running around a curve, waving his arms and shouting:

"Stop! Stop!"

CHAPTER XXIV

FREDDIE'S BIG SPLASH

MR. BOBBSEY brought the auto to a stop in the middle of the road while the excited man, still waving his arms, kept on running toward it.

"What does he want?" asked Bert in a low voice.

"That's what I'm going to find out," said his father. He looked sharply at the man as if he did not quite like what was happening.

"Oh," exclaimed Flossie, "maybe he's found our dog and wants to give him back to us!"

"Wouldn't that be wonderful!" cried Freddie.

"Don't be silly!" murmured Nan. "We never saw this man before and I don't believe he ever saw us, so how could he know that we had lost a dog?"

"Well, maybe he does!" insisted Flossie.

The small twins were ready to believe anything when it came to finding Waggo.

Meanwhile the running, shouting man had reached the auto which Mr. Bobbsey had stopped.

"What's the matter?" asked the parent of the twins.

"You can't go any farther on this road."

"Why not?"

"Because the bridge is broken. It just happened—not five minutes ago. A big truck went over it and cracked some of the beams."

"Then I can't get to Highfield on this road?" asked Mr. Bobbsey.

"No, you'll have to turn back and go through Midvale. That's the nearest bridge over the river."

"But that is many miles out of the way. I can hardly get to Highfield that way before dark, and it looks," said Mr. Bobbsey, gazing at the sky, "as if a storm were coming."

"Yes, I think it's going to storm," said the man. "It's too bad, but it can't be helped."

"Did a circus truck break the bridge?" asked Freddie.

"No, it was an oil truck," the man explained. "What made you think it was a circus truck?"

"Oh, these children of mine have had a lot to do with a circus lately," Mr. Bobbsey explained. "They've lost a dog and we've been to the show in Greenberg thinking we might find their pet. But we didn't, so now we're on our way home to Lakeport."

"You have a good distance to go," said the man as Mr. Bobbsey told the story of the missing Waggo. "I'm surely sorry about your dog, children."

"May we go see the broken bridge?" asked Freddie.

"No, we can't take the time," his father answered. He turned the car and the Bobbsey twins, still mourning for the lost Waggo, started on the new route to Lakeport and their home.

The sky, which had begun to cloud up soon after they had left Greenberg, was now getting very dark. The wind began to blow in fitful gusts and Mr. Bobbsey cast more than one anxious look toward the dark masses of clouds in the west.

"It will storm soon, I'm afraid," he said.

"What can we do?" asked Bert. "Shall I get out the side curtains?"

"Perhaps you had better," his father agreed. "We'll stop at the first garage we come to and put them up. If I drive fast I may get to Rockford before the rain comes." Rockford was the next town on the roundabout way to Midvale where the nearest bridge was to be found.

The storm suddenly broke before they had traveled another mile. There was no sheltering garage in sight, so Mr. Bobbsey stopped the car beneath a big, spreading maple tree beside the road. With Bert helping, he adjusted the side curtains with their celluloid windows.

Mr. Bobbsey and Bert got rather wet doing this, but they did not mind since the curtains gave protection to Nan and the small twins. Freddie was eager to get out and help but Nan made him stay inside the car.

"There! I guess we can get to Rockford without much more trouble," Mr. Bobbsey said as they started off again. "There's a hotel there. How good it is I don't know, but we'll have to stay there all night. I don't want to drive after dark in this storm. I think it will be much worse by morning."

"Will Mother be all right?" Flossie wanted to know.

"Oh, yes," her father said with a smile.

On and on through the wind and rain Mr. Bobbsey drove. Even with the windshield wiper working at top speed, the water was so thick on the glass at times that Mr. Bobbsey could hardly see where he was driving. In spite of the side curtains, the rain dashed in and sprayed the children but they did not really mind it much.

Suddenly Freddie, who was now in front with his father and Bert, pointed through the windshield and cried:

"Oh, look!"

"What?" asked Bert.

"See that big puddle!" went on Freddie. "Are we going through that, Daddy?"

"I think we must if we are to reach shelter," answered Mr. Bobbsey. He looked carefully at the dirt road which was now very muddy from the rain. The highway was soft and it was hard going for the auto. More than once the wheels sank down into ruts and it was only by using more power that Mr. Bobbsey pulled out of the sticky places.

"Maybe it's a deep puddle," suggested Freddie.

"We'll soon know," his father said. Into the water, with a big splash, the auto ran. A quarter way through the car slowed up, and halfway through it slowed still more. Mr. Bobbsey pressed the gas pedal as far down as it would go, but it was of no use. The car came to a standstill a little way beyond the halfway mark in the big, muddy puddle.

"What's the matter?" called Nan from the rear seat.

"I'm afraid we're stalled," her father answered. "But I'll shift to low gear and try to pull out."

He moved the lever, the rubber-tired wheels churned around in the mud and water, throwing up a brown spray, but the car did not move.

"We're stuck!" Bert exclaimed.

"Oh!" murmured Nan.

"Will we have to stay here all night?" faltered Flossie.

"We can't stay here," Freddie said.

Again Mr. Bobbsey tried to drive the car out of the sticky mudhole, but it never moved. Bert opened the door on his side to lean out and look at the puddle.

"It's a deep one," he said.

"Let me see," begged Freddie, leaning toward his brother.

"Careful, or you'll fall out, Freddie!" cautioned Nan again.

"No, I won't fall," answered the little boy.

"There's a farmhouse just down the road," Bert reported as he peered through the rain.

"I'm afraid we can't make it," answered Mr. Bobbsey. "We are too deep in the mud. But perhaps I can get the farmer to haul us out with his team or his auto if he has one. I'll walk down there and ask him."

"Be careful, Freddie," warned his father, for the little boy was leaning farther over toward the open door to see what Bert was looking at. Freddie's hand accidentally touched the horn button on the steering wheel and sent a loud blast honking through the air.

"Oh," exclaimed the little boy. "I didn't mean to do that."

Following the tooting of the horn a dog was heard to bark. A moment later the dog itself came running down the muddy road from the direction of the farmhouse. Bert took one look at the dog and exclaimed:

"Why, it's Waggo!"

"Waggo!" cried Nan. "You mean our lost dog?"

"Sure!" Bert answered. "There he is! There's Waggo!" The dog came nearer, still barking, disturbed probably, by the honking of the horn.

"Yes, it *is* Waggo!" shouted Freddie, leaning farther over toward the open door. "But look at his paw! It's hurt! It's tied up in a rag."

"Oh, poor Waggo!" murmured Flossie as she, too, saw the limping animal. For the dog, wet and bedraggled, that was running toward the Bobbsey twins, and barking, held up a bandaged front paw.

"How in the world did Waggo get here?" asked Nan.

"He must have been in that farmhouse," suggested Bert.

"Are you sure it's Waggo?" asked Mr. Bobbsey.

"Oh, sure!" Bert answered, and the other children were, also.

"Oh, Freddie, do be careful!" warned Nan. "You'll fall! Don't lean out so far!"

The warning came too late. In another instant Freddie, in his eagerness to see Waggo, slipped out of the auto and fell into the mud puddle with a big splash.

CHAPTER XXV

THE CHILDREN'S CIRCUS

BERT BOBBSEY jumped out on the running-board, reached down into the puddle and lifted Freddie up before much harm could happen to the little fellow. But though poor Freddie was not hurt he was covered with mud and water from head to foot.

"Oh, Freddie!" exclaimed his father.

"What did you do it for?" asked Nan.

"I—I didn't—do it!" spluttered Freddie. "I—I couldn't help it! I—I—slipped!"

"Yes, he slipped all right," Bert said. "Stand still, Freddie, on the running-board for a minute, until some of the mud drips off of you. We don't want to get the car all dirty."

"Oh, never mind the car! Lift him in!" said Mr. Bobbsey.

This Bert did, using his handkerchief to wipe some of the mud and water off his brother's face. Freddie was wet through and very dirty. But in spite of this he looked toward the side of the road, and pointing to the barking dog cried:

"It is Waggo! It is! See!"

There was now no question about it—there was the missing pet dog. And when he heard his name called by the Bobbsey twins he stopped barking, joyfully wagged his tail and tried to climb into the auto, half swimming, half wading through the puddle. But he could not get up on the running-board.

"It's his poor, lame paw!" cried Nan. "Oh, Waggo!"

"I guess he'll never be able to do circus tricks now," spoke Flossie, half crying.

"Oh, I think his paw can be made well," said Mr. Bobbsey. "I'm glad you have your dog back. But what are we going to do about Freddie? He must have dry clothes."

Bert reached down, lifted Waggo, wet and muddy as he was, into the car, and then a voice hailed the party.

"Are you folks in trouble?" asked a big farmer in rubber boots and a rain-coat. He had come down the road from the house Bert had seen.

"Yes, we are in a bit of trouble," Mr. Bobbsey answered. "We're stuck in the mud."

"And I fell in, but I don't care 'cause we've got Waggo back!" exclaimed Freddie as the farmer came to the side of the car.

"Oh, is that your dog?" asked Mr. Yardley, as he introduced himself, and learned the name of the father of the twins. "We thought he must belong to somebody. I'll tell you how we got him after I haul your car out of the mud, I'll be back in a little while, Mr. Bobbsey," he said. "I'll go get my car."

In a short time the Bobbsey auto was hauled out of the hole by the farmer's car, after which he insisted on the family coming into his house to rest and get dry.

"You'd better not try to go on in this storm," Mr. Yardley said when they were in the warm, dry kitchen of the farmhouse. "It's going to be worse, and that little fellow might catch cold, for he's wet through."

"Yes, he is," agreed Mr. Bobbsey. "I should like to have him change his clothes. I have a dry suit in the valise."

"Then stay all night," invited Mrs. Yardley "We have plenty of room. Tomorrow the storm may stop, and you could go on then."

"And will you tell us how you got our dog Waggo?" asked Bert.

"Well, there isn't much to tell," said the farmer with a laugh, when Freddie had on dry clothes. "The dog came to us some time ago. We didn't know his name, nor where he came from. But from the fact that there was a piece of rope, with a frayed end, about his neck, I guessed that he must have been tied in some auto and broken loose. He must have jumped out and that's how he hurt his paw.

"Anyhow, he came limping to our house and my wife and I took him in. She bandaged his paw and it's mending now. 'Tisn't as sore as it was."

"That's good!" murmured Freddie. "Then I guess he can do tricks in the circus."

"What circus?" asked the farmer. "Is he a circus dog?"

"Sort of," Bert said, and Flossie added:

"He's going to be in a circus we're going to have."

"Oh, I see!" laughed the farmer. "Well, I guess his paw will soon be well enough so he can do tricks. He's a smart dog, I knew that the moment I first saw him. He has a great habit of running out to bark every time he hears an auto horn. He heard one a while ago and ran out in the rain, though I tried to stop him."

"I blew the horn, but I didn't mean to. Now I'm glad I did," announced Freddie.

"Well, I came out to get the dog and so I happened to see you," said Mr. Yardley.

"It's a good thing you did," remarked Mr. Bobbsey.

The next day the storm cleared, and with many thanks to the kind farmer and his wife, the Bobbsey twins, taking Waggo with them, started back home. It was a joyful journey. They could only guess where Waggo had been before reaching the farmhouse. They never found out.

Mrs. Bobbsey welcomed her family home, and was glad they had found Waggo. Even Snap seemed pleased to meet his dog friend and the two rubbed noses and wagged tails.

After a week or two, during which time Waggo's paw healed, the Bobbsey twins began to train their pets in tricks for the circus. Snap was hard to teach, but Waggo more than made up for him. At last the day came for the children's circus. A tent was put up in the back yard and many boys and girls, and not a few grown-ups, paid money to see the performance.

Waggo, Snap, Snoop and the Christmas cat did all the tricks they had been taught, and there was much laughter, when in the middle of one trick, Snap became tired and walked right off the stage. He did not come back, either. But Waggo was fine. Not only did he do the tricks of shaking paws, climbing up a ladder and playing "dead dog," but he drummed with his tail on a real drum that Bert found up in the attic.

The best, though, was when a tub, filled with water, was placed on a chair, and one of Flossie's old dolls thrown in. At once Waggo leaped into the water and "rescued" the doll. The audience laughed and applauded. Then Waggo shook himself free of water, walked about on his hind legs, and as a closing stunt to the act left the stage, turning one somersault after another.

It was a jolly circus and everyone was pleased, and most of all the Bobbsey twins.

"Waggo is a grand dog!" exclaimed Freddie, and the other children agreed with him.

They wanted to take him many places to show him off, but sometimes their parents could not allow this. One of these times was on a journey into the sky. It is called "The Bobbsey Twins on an Airplane Trip."

Jolly and exciting days were ahead of them, but never would they forget the fun they had just had.

"I love circuses," said Flossie.

"And 'specially our own," added Freddie.

THE END